THE SILVER MOON MASSACRE

Ezra Unbound

Book Two

SAMANTHA HUFFMAN

IBSN: 979-8-9927327-2-6

Author: Samantha Huffman
Illustrations by: Kaylan S.
Cover design by: Muhammad Waqas
Copy Editing by: English Proper Editing Services
Printed in the United States of America

Luna

Dedication

In honor of *my* Junior Black.

The day you walked into my life, everything changed. You've

been everything since that moment, my biggest "Hype" guy, my

shoulder to lean on, my safe place, and some things I can't name

to the public.

"I Ahem, Ahem, Ahem You."

Thank You, Punky.

Trigger Warnings

Childhood Abuse (Physical/Sexual

Memories On/Off PAGE)

Explicit Language

Violence, Torture

Un-Aliving of People (On PAGE)

Explicit Sexual Scenes

Non/Con

Dub/Con

Knife-Play

Breath-Play

BDSM

ANAL

Sexual Over-stimulation

Accidental Pregnancy

Loss of a love one to Cancer

CONTENTS

CHAPTER ONE

This Ends Now

Ezra's POV

Gabe's voice sliced through the chaos around us, and I froze. Every moment that had led up to tonight played through my mind, whispers of all the memories lost.

Time with Bash that I would *never* get back.

"In the depths of the morning, as the sun begins to rise, I think of you, dear Ezra, and those bright, blue eyes. You will never walk alone, for I will guide your stride, you and me together, side by side."

It was as if the very fabric of reality was unraveling, revealing a glimpse into something darker. Zayne was pulling me relentlessly toward the main gate, but my feet were cemented to the ground, refusing to relinquish an inch to his urgent tugging.

The dread in the air all but clung to my skin, chilling me to the bone. The shadows danced with a life of their own as screams echoed throughout the campus grounds.

Zayne shook me hard. "Ezra, we have to move!"

I looked down at my hands and chest; the blood of my mate, which still covered me, was less vibrant now. It was beginning to harden and crack as I curled my fingers into hard fists. The blood pumping through my veins burned with a hatred I didn't know I could feel, encasing my heart within its fiery tomb.

Gabe sang those familiar words, and every note was a taunting reminder of the betrayal and the blood on his hands. Bash's death would be his most profound regret. Gabe would pay for what he'd taken from me, and that song would be his requiem.

Spinning on my heels, I yanked free of Zayne's grip and rushed towards Gabe. "You're fucking dead, you hear me?!"

His grin widened, exposing his canines, as he stood there singing the song he'd written for me all that time ago—the song that once melted my heart had become the bellows that stoked the fires of my ire, each gust of emotion a dark verse in the ballad of my bitterness.

He spread his hands out toward the silver moon above us, singing, "I want to dance with you in the silver glow of the moon, as the world fades away, in a dream come true."

The heat within was almost unbearable now as I continued closing the distance between us. In what world is any of this a dream come true?! How could all these deaths be seen as anything other than an awful waste? This was a goddamn tragedy; this was fucking HELL!

He continued singing, "You are mine, sweet love; together, we'll soar high, but ***only with me*** will you touch the endless sky. In this journey of love, with every step we trace, know it's you, dear Ezra, who belongs in my embrace."

The memories of Gabe's possessiveness, mixed with the intensity of what he had just done to Bash, seemed to trigger something within me—an internal storm of such ferocity that I lost all control. All sane thoughts evaporated as I approached that devil incarnate. "How dare you! You can't control me anymore, Gabe. I'm not yours to command."

"Oh, but you are, kitten; I won you fair and square."

Anger surged through me, pure and menacing.

"You killed my mate! That wins you nothing besides a one-way trip to hell!"

As I moved towards him, I grabbed a sword from the fighting racks. I might suck at existing, but until my last breath, I would fight. I've been fighting my whole life. So, if it's the last thing I do, I'm going to ruin this asshole.

Gabe's eyes widened with a hint of surprise, and his inflated ego tumbled from his mouth. "Submit to me, Ezra. Before you hurt yourself, we both know you aren't strong enough to fight this. You submit, and nobody else needs to die."

"You're wrong," I sneered as I took a fighting stance. "One more person is going to die today, and it's going to be you!"

"Ezra," Zayne pleaded from behind me. I honestly had forgotten all about him, but if he thought I would back down after everything this bastard put me through, he was sorely mistaken.

"You can help your Luna avenge our Alpha, or you can go, Zayne. Either way, I'm going to kill him," I assured him, never taking my eyes off Gabe. My grip tightened around the hilt of the blade as my breath came in ragged gasps, every inhale a testament to the years of struggle I had already faced. Gabe stood directly across from me, a sneer twisting his lips.

"You think you can take me down, Ezra? Even your Alpha couldn't beat me," he taunted, his voice dripping with disdain.

"You cheated. If Thomas hadn't attacked me, Bash would be alive instead of you. We both know it." My eyes narrowed, a fierce determination blazing within them. "Besides, I know how much you love punishments, Gabe. I think it's well past time for you to get what's coming to you."

I lunged forward, swinging the sword with all the force I could muster. My lack of general know-how with a sword allowed Gabe to parry the blow effortlessly. I let out a growl of exasperation, but refused to back down. I struck again and again, each attack fueled by a lifetime of pent-up frustration and pain.

Gabe countered, sending me sprawling to the ground as the hilt of his sword smashed into my cheek.

"This is a waste of time," he said, holding out his hand to me.

Smacking it away, I scrambled to my feet. Blood was trickling down from the fresh cut under my eye, but I readied myself to face him again.

Zayne stepped in, attacking from Gabe's left, but he deflected the blow easily and countered with a strike of his own, the sword slicing through Zayne's shoulder blade.

"This ends now," I growled, my voice low and menacing.

Gabe laughed, but there was a flicker of uncertainty in his eyes as Zayne shifted his sword to his uninjured arm, nodding at me. Two against one. I like those odds.

"You're outmatched, Ezra. Just give up. I'll even forgive your little temper tantrum and make you a Luna again."

"I'll never be *your* Luna," I spat as I relaunched myself at him, Zayne shadowing my movements from the side. The clash of steel rang out as all four swords met, a symphony of violence and desperation.

He might be physically stronger, but he underestimated my resolve, which remained unbreakable. I fought with everything I had; nothing else mattered in that moment. I wanted the life of the man who had just stolen mine.

By some stroke of luck, I had managed to disarm Gabe with my next strike, his sword clattering to the ground. He stumbled back, clutching his remaining sword, his confidence now wavering.

Zayne moved to strike again, but I held up my hand, "Please, Zayne. Let me do this."

Reluctantly, Zayne lowered his sword and, with a slight nod, stepped back.

"This is for every time you made me feel worthless," I said, my voice trembling, my body completely exhausted as I swung my sword. He blocked it and stumbled back further, his eyes scanning the area around us. "And this is for trying to force me to have your fucking pup!" I swung again, another block, another step backward.

My breath was forced and staggered. I took a deep breath and forced out the following phrase, "And this is for my mate!" I lunged the sword forward, but he couldn't retreat any further. His back was to the wall, and as the sword tore through his flesh, he looked at me with such disdain. I didn't realize just how much I had changed until this moment. But in truth, I wasn't the same girl I used to be, and while he hated me for it, I had never felt stronger.

When he pulled the sword from his stomach, the sound of metal on the cobblestone was somehow the most satisfying sound I'd ever heard.

In an instant, he shifted and ran off. I didn't kill him…*yet*, but maybe he would do us all a favor and bleed out. Zayne started after him, but I stopped him.

"Let him go, we need to get the remaining members of our pack to safety."

Staring at the blood-stained sword on the ground before me, I knelt down and picked it up. As I wiped the blade against my thighs to clean it, there was a shift in me. I was no longer a scared little girl. I was Night Tree Pack's Luna; I was a fighter. This was far from over, but I had a purpose now.

Zayne draped his arm over my shoulder in a half-hug as he squeezed me into his side. It was as casual, as if we'd been best friends our whole lives—but somehow, it just worked.

"He'd be proud, Ezra," he whispered as he pulled me in closer.

Zayne and I had never really talked. I knew he was Bash's best friend, his Beta, but I had never really gotten to know him. All I knew was that he saved me today; whether that was for Bash or me, I owed him my life.

"Come on; we have work to do. Let's move any remaining pack members to the pack house. We need to get the wounded care and assess the damage our pack sustained tonight, before the cops show up."

"A lot of them submitted and left with Silver Pack," Zayne replied, motioning to the remains of the college, which was now in ruins, with bodies on bodies of fallen wolves from both packs.

I wasn't exactly sure how we were going to clean up this mess. I'm sure the cover story would be something absurd like a hazmat truck that lost control, busted through the barricades, and exploded in the center of the college.

As stupid as that sounded, normies would believe it. I swear, humans would believe anything so that they could ignore the reality that our kind existed.

"No doubt, they did what they thought would save them, but they are not traitors, Zayne. They are victims just like you and me. Like…Bash." I sighed. The pain of losing him was so fresh, and I didn't have the luxury of time to grieve. "I was his Luna, and I'm going to free them. Next time, Gabe won't get away from me."

"The Elders spoke of the One True Alpha. Who knew today would bring us a fierce Luna in his place? I will stand with you, Ezra, if you'd have me." He bowed slightly, and I offered him a pat on his shoulder in return.

"I couldn't think of anyone better suited."

"We stick together, for Bash."

"For Bash," I agreed as I moved to the center of the courtyard and knelt next to his body. Closing his eyes, I ran my fingers down his face and placed one last kiss on his forehead. All the warmth of him had long faded. "I love you, too," I whispered, turning to the moon.

I could hear Lana's faint whimpers, her pain and agony echoing my sorrow. But I couldn't bring myself to mourn his loss. Mourning Bash meant accepting that there was now a world where he no longer existed. The idea of a reality where his laughter was nothing more than a phantom echo, or his warmth, a forgotten sun, was something I couldn't process.

Instead, I chose defiance. A fierce refusal to let the void swallow his memory. Clinging to the fragments of yesterday as if they were stars in this desolate night sky.

As the silver moon above us cast shadows around us, Zayne's wolf lifted its nuzzle to the Moon Goddess and howled. After his first howl, a chorus joined in—a symphony in honor of our fallen Alpha.

Tears blurred my vision as I walked away, each note and every howl piercing my heart. The pack's voices melded together, creating a haunting melody that reverberated through the night—a tribute to our lost leader.

I felt the weight of their grief, the sorrow of their loss, and the unity of what remained of our pack. The howls grew louder and more desperate, as if trying to reach the heavens and bring our Alpha back. But deep down, I'm sure we all knew that he was gone. As the final notes faded into the stillness, the silence that followed was deafening.

CHAPTER TWO

Not Everyone's Luna

Ezra's POV

"Quick, over here!" I yelled as two more wounded were brought into the infirmary.

"Ezra—" the nurse began, but Zayne interrupted her.

"That's our Luna, show some respect."

"My apologies," she said. "My Luna, we don't have any more open beds…there are just too many wounded."

"It's fine," I said, shooting Zayne a *would you chill?* look. "What if we set up a temporary med bay in the dining hall…the most critical will remain in the infirmary, and those with minor injuries should be moved there. For now, find space wherever you can," I commanded. "Use the gathering hall, the training rooms—anywhere with enough room to lay them down."

"Yes, Luna…but then there is staffing. We aren't equipped to deal with patients of this magnitude."

"We have to make it work…" A loud beeping sound echoed in the halls, and another nurse turned the corner. "This one's crashing!" she yelled.

Shit.

As the nurse before me took off running down the hall, I helped the two new men down onto the beds, which were pushed against the wall in the infirmary hallway.

"Hey, I see you've got a pretty bad cut here. Anything else we need to look at?" I asked.

"No, Luna, it'll take more than this to break me," the first man replied, and I offered him a quick, warm smile.

"I'm okay, too," the other man assured me, "but my shoulder hurts; I think it might be dislocated."

"I'll have the nurse look at you as soon as possible; just hang in there, okay? Excuse me just a moment, please."

My heart was pounding with a rhythm that matched the frantic pace of the scene around me. The infirmary was overflowing. The air was thick with the scent of blood and the moans of the wounded.

I moved through the halls with what I can only describe as determination. I prayed to the Moon Goddess to please offer me some sense of direction here.

Bash made me Luna, but I wondered if my presence here would offer a beacon of hope amidst the despair, or if my pack would blame me for the loss of our Alpha. That blame would hardly be misplaced. If it weren't for me, none of this would have happened.

I knelt beside a young warrior. His face was pale, and his eyes were glazed over with pain. I reached out, touching his forehead gently. "Stay with me," I whispered. "We will get through this night together."

I knew this was my responsibility as Luna, so I moved tirelessly, helping however I could. I organized supplies, offered words of comfort, and ensured that no one was left unattended. But the nurse were right; we were understaffed.

I entered the dining hall, where most of the pack was gathered. "We need volunteers," I called out, and I was surprised by the authority that rang out. "If anyone here has basic first aid knowledge, please step forward. We must work together to get through this."

At first, everyone continued to talk and murmur amongst themselves. My fears were obviously justified, as I clearly had no authority in this matter. I didn't even know most of these people. I had spent my whole life as a prisoner in my dad's home. I rarely attended pack events, and if I had not met Bash...I wouldn't even be their Luna.

"Quiet down!" Zayne yelled at my side. Soon, the murmurs began to die down, and then he continued. "We are more than just a pack. We are a family. And tonight, we need to care for our own. Who will help us?" He had found his way back to my side, and I was thankful that he was here. The pack knew him, and they respected him.

Pack members, young and old, began to step up, their faces set with determination. I assigned tasks to them based on their knowledge and skill set. Those without expertise were tasked with setting up a triage in the gathering hall and moving anyone with minor injuries there.

I nudged Zayne on the shoulder. "Thank you."

"Of course, don't worry about it. Eventually, they'll all come around," he assured me as he trotted off to help out.

With each passing moment, the chaos seemed to dissipate, the disorder transforming into a coordinated effort to save our packmates. That night seemed to stretch on forever. I'm happy to say we lost very few, but we couldn't save everyone, and those losses will always haunt me.

At one point, I saw Elder John. Unsure of what to say, I quickly turned my attention away from him and back to my current task.

How do you tell the father of the man you love *I'm sorry that your son passed away fighting in my honor, and that I was the distraction that cost him his life?*

"Ezzie!" I heard a familiar voice behind me, and for the first time the whole night, I felt some sense of calmness myself.

"KIT!" I exclaimed as I turned around just in time for her to smash into me with the biggest hug she'd probably ever given me. Her family was behind her, and I was relieved that they were all okay.

"Ezzie, babes, don't take this the wrong way, but you seriously look like shit. You should take a break and get some sleep."

"Is there a right way to take that?" I laughed. "Besides, I'm okay. I'll sleep when I know everyone is going to be okay," I said, but like clockwork, Zayne approached.

"You know she's right. You really should get some rest. If we need you, I'll come get you," he said, agreeing with her, and the looks on both of their faces told me I wouldn't win this one.

"There is still so much to do. We need to get a roster of our remaining pack members, assign rooms, and get everyone settled in. And it's been a long night. We should really get food in everyone's stomachs. Were the cooks we had on staff still here? I can't sleep. Not yet. There is just too much to do."

"We can handle it," Zayne said, turning me and pushing me towards the doors that led to the main hall.

"I can't, I'll just…I'll rest here," I argued. The last thing I wanted to do was go to our room…everything would be exactly as Bash left it yesterday morning. And I couldn't let myself think about him right now. Being in that room wouldn't allow me to rest. It would only bring me the reality I had been trying hard to forget all night. That the love of my life. My Alpha. My mate…was gone.

With a smile, as if he were treading lightly, Zayne said, "You can all stay in my room tonight; we'll figure everything else out after you've rested, Luna. Besides, if anyone here deserves a break, it's you. The nurses still aren't sure how you even lived through last night's events."

"It's not unheard of. It was just unlikely to live after—"

Kit's arms were around me before I could finish that sentence, and I was reminded why I could not live without this girl. She was always there, and I also owed her safety to Zayne. He got her out of there. Another debt to this guy whom I barely knew, but was suddenly relying on in more ways than one.

"Are you sure?" I asked this unexpected friend. Can I call him a friend after one night? Honestly, with the current situation, I could use all the friends I could get. And if Bash trusted him indefinitely, I would, too.

"Yeah, absolutely." He waved over a guard, instructing him to take us to his room and get us settled in.

Walking into his room, I suddenly missed Bash's overly organized bedroom. The amount of disorganized crazy in this room made me laugh.

"How can anyone live like this?" Kit asked as she took in the room of my Beta.

The clutter in his room defied all notions of order. The bed was buried beneath a mountain of crumpled, black, band t-shirts and ripped jeans. Books were spread out all along the floor, their pages splayed open as if they were gasping for air.

Half-empty cups and forgotten snacks covered nearly every surface, looking like they had long since surrendered to the march of time. The desk groaned under the weight of abandoned projects, tangled cables, and a forest of miscellaneous electronics that had lost their way.

Posters hung askew on the walls, their edges curling in resignation, while the floor was a minefield of discarded skate shoes and rogue socks. Five—no, six—skateboards were hanging on the far wall, and a stack of hats was piled on the chair in the corner.

"Well, on the bright side, it's quiet in here." I laughed.

The guard left momentarily and returned with some clean sheets and blankets. After we cleared the bed and put fresh sheets on it, I felt more at ease. Kit and I picked up all the books and placed them back on the bookshelf.

Making beds on the floor for ourselves while her parents took the bed. I was exhausted, and it didn't take long for me to fall asleep. My head lay cocooned on Kit's shoulder, and she was petting my head the same way she'd put me to sleep for years.

I don't know when we finally fell asleep, but I woke up well after two in the afternoon. I must have been way more tired than I thought, and waking up in Zayne's room had left me dazed and confused.

"Kit?" I asked, and she emerged from the bathroom. Zayne's room had been cleaned from top to bottom.

"Oh, hey!" she said, coming to sit by me. I had been moved up onto the bed, and her parents were long gone.

"How long have you been up?" I asked, taking in the freshly cleaned bedroom.

"Just a few hours. I hope he doesn't mind, but this room desperately needed a woman's touch." She laughed.

"You've been busy, it looks about a thousand times better in here."

"I know, right?!" she exclaimed. "Here. I had some clothes brought up for you. Why don't you go shower and get dressed, and we can get you some food? They made lunch for everyone, and it looks so good! I wanted to wait for you so we could eat together!"

"Thanks, Kit. You really are the best!"

"Duh. Now get ready!"

It didn't take long to get to the dining hall. Walking in was like being the new kid at a new school, starting mid-year. Everyone's eyes seemed to land on me, and I hated every second of it. There was absolutely no blending anymore, not for me.

I tried greeting everyone with warm, friendly smiles. But moving among the people gathered there, I couldn't help but overhear some of the comments.

"It's her *fault."*

"I can't believe Bash died *for her."*

"The bond should have killed her! *At least then, Zayne would be in charge."*

"She'll never *be my Luna."*

"Maybe we should have defected to Silver Pack…"

What's worse than being the new kid in a new school, starting mid-year, you might ask? Being that kid and having everyone hate you. What was Bash thinking? I cannot be the Luna of this pack.

"Just ignore them," Kit whispered beside me.

Zayne came running up to greet us. "Good morning, Luna!"

"Hardly," I muttered.

"Hey, it's Kit…right?"

"The one and only," Kit laughed.

I was finding it somewhat annoying how happy these two were, how could they be laughing when literally everything sucked. If I could have disappeared today, I would have. It wasn't like the pack was wrong about any of it. They weren't saying anything I hadn't already thought myself. I had ruined a century-long era of peace because I was afraid of love. It *was* my fault, and I *should* have died with Bash.

"Eventually, they will see the same thing Bash did. It's the same thing I see now. It will just take some time. Did you rest enough? Are you hungry?" He pulled me into a hug suddenly. And I gave him an intensely awkward pat on the back. I don't think I'll ever get used to this whole hugging thing.

"Ezra, you *are* our Luna," he affirmed as he released me from that awkward embrace.

"Not everyone's Luna," I said. "But I am starving, so yes, can we please eat?"

"Yeah, let's get you some food, and then we can discuss sleeping arrangements, etc. Also, we have a formal count of our remaining members."

"Sounds great. Thank you, Zayne."

"It's no problem. I'm glad to have the distraction. You know, with everything."

Yeah, I know.

After a moment of silence, Zayne continued. "Bash always had this way of making everything seem possible, you know. I will carry that same hope for you, Ez. For all of us."

"He saved me—more times than I can count in such a short time. We have to save this pack now. He wouldn't have wanted everything to be lost. That…would make his death meaningless, and I can't accept that."

"We will. But first—food. So, what do you want? There's grilled cheese with tomato soup or chicken Caesar wraps with a side of sweet potato fries."

"Maybe the wrap?"

"Cool, our table is over there." He pointed to the table at the head of the dining hall. "I'll be right back."

"Great." But it wasn't great. As if they didn't hate me enough already, now I have to sit at the head of the dining hall, where nobody thinks I deserve to be.

I forced a deep breath. *What was I thinking? What had Bash been thinking?* He believed I would be the best Luna for our pack, but now it was time for me to prove it. He really did have a way of making everything seem possible. I was actually starting to believe that with him, I maybe could be a good Luna. I'm feeling way less optimistic now.

More disgusting comments were made while I made my way to the table. Justified or not, I couldn't let this continue. I set my stuff down and made my way to the stage. I felt like I was going to throw up. The adrenaline from last night has long since faded, and the thought of addressing the pack was overwhelmingly terrifying.

Public speaking, in general, wasn't something I had ever excelled at. Actually, until this last summer, speaking to anyone except Kit was difficult for me. I closed my eyes. *Please help me, Bash.*

"You've got this," Lana said, encouraging me to follow through with this obnoxious plan of mine.

I took another deep breath, grabbed the microphone, and stepped onto the stage.

"Night Tree Pack, if I could please have your attention for a moment, I have something I'd like to say."

Some of them were kind enough to give me their attention; but the abundance of rolling eyes, scoffs, and lack of respect vastly outweighed them.

"Don't let them walk over you. You're a Luna. Command their attention."

"LISTEN UP!" I said into the microphone, adding as much bass as possible to my voice. It worked, and everyone looked my way as the room fell silent. As I stood there, all eyes on me, the weight of their loss hung heavy in the air. I softened my tone as I spoke again.

"Beloved Night Tree Pack," I began, my eyes sweeping over the gathered wolves, "we stand now in the shadow of a great loss. Our Alpha, our guide, our protector, has left us. His absence is a wound that we all feel deeply, a void that seems impossible to fill."

I paused, fighting back the tears. *Strength*. That's what this pack needs right now. "It's in this darkness that we must find our light. Our Alpha believed in every one of us. He saw the strength, the courage, and the unity that binds us together. In his honor, we must now rise, not as individuals, but as a family."

"You're doing well. Keep going." Lana urged.

My gaze grew fiercer, my voice unwavering. "There is unrest among us, a fear of the unknown future. Some are questioning our fallen Alpha's choice of mate. But I will say this: our future is not written in the stars; our own hands forge it. Together, we will honor his legacy by standing strong, supporting one another, and facing the approaching war with the same bravery he taught us the night of the silver moon."

I took another deep breath as I paced the stage, my heart beating frantically in my chest. "I see a future where we thrive, where our bonds are unbreakable, and our spirits unyielding. We will mourn, yes, but we will also heal. We will rise from that grief a stronger pack."

My voice softened once more, a gentle plea to their hearts. "I ask you to trust in me, as he trusted in us. Let us walk this path together, hand in hand, heart to heart. For in our unity, we will find our strength, and in that strength, we will find our future."

Satisfied, I turned off the mic and walked off the stage. As I reached our table, Elder John's eyes met mine. They conveyed a mixture of grief and perhaps pride. A silent acknowledgment of the heavy burden I now carry. It was one thing to stand as Luna at Bash's side. But the promise I made tonight held within it a responsibility to honor Bash's legacy, and to lead the pack with the same courage and wisdom that he would have.

In the depths, I saw the echoes of the past, the legacy of leadership, and the sacrifice that his son embodied. Maybe there was a glimmer of hope in them, a quiet but steadfast belief in my ability to guide the pack through these tumultuous times.

Or maybe it was simply an unspoken language of a shared loss and a shared future, but it resonated deeply with me. I may have lost my mate, the only man I had ever loved, but he had lost his son. I could never imagine the level of grief that would accompany that loss.

Chapter Three

For The Sake of The Pack

Ezra's POV

It's been one week since "The Silver Moon Massacre." Or at least that's the name that keeps circling through our pack after my speech. The Night Tree pack once had a total of over a hundred members. The final tally of those who remained is now forty-six, and quite a few of them were injured. The death count was twenty-four from our pack alone. This means about thirty of our members submitted to Silver Pack.

Of course, on the bright side, one of the deserters was my father. So now, I had two targets: the one who haunted my past and the one who had stolen my future.

"They think they can hide, but a pack always finds its prey." Lana's voice was low and menacing as she spoke.

"Simmer, Lana. Right now, it's our pack that is hiding. It's too soon to ask any of our injured people to fight, and it will take Gabe a while to heal to a point where he can attack us, so for a moment, we are safe."

"Wolves do not hide. They circle their prey and strike!" she snapped back at me.

"Not when they are outnumbered, outmatched, and already wounded, they don't! Running in there all willy-nilly and without a plan could cost us what's left of our pack!" I was pacing the room now, mentally scrunching my brain as if I could squeeze an idea out of it.

"If they die, they will die with their honor."

"Well, why don't we find a way not to die instead? And if you aren't going to help, then please be quiet so I can think."

"Stubborn human."

"Foolish wolf," I snapped back before pushing Lana to the back of my mind. I was looking out the big window of Bash's bedroom when I heard a knock on the door.

"Ezra?"

It was Zayne. He was checking in on me again. I wasn't sure why he cared so much, but as obnoxious as it sometimes seemed, I was happy to have him here.

"Come in," I said, trying to steady my voice. Zayne entered, his eyes filled with so much sorrow and concern that they pained my heart.

"What's wrong?" Zayne asked gently, his voice barely above a whisper.

I sighed, shouldering the burden of the situation pressing down on me. "I just need a moment to figure things out. Everything's so chaotic. I have no idea how to run a pack, and everything just feels so fucked. Like

I'm…like I'm completely naïve about this," I admitted, my voice trembling. "I don't even know where to start."

Zayne nodded; his presence was a comforting anchor in the storm of my thoughts. "We're all here for you, Ezra. We'll get through this together."

Not everyone…

I looked at him, grateful for his unwavering support. "Thanks, Zayne. I needed to hear that."

"And you do have Elders here…Bash's father is still here, and mine."

"Elder John is mourning the loss of his son, as he should be, not planning for a war that, at this point? I'm not sure we have a chance in hell of winning."

"He'd want to help. And do I need to remind you? We both lost him, too." He pulled me into another hug. It was something he seemed to do every time he brought up Bash. I guess it was his way of softening the blow whenever he brought him up, afraid I might break all over again.

"I know. I'm fine, Zayne," I said, wiggling out of his embrace.

"I see that, my Luna. You are every bit as strong as he claimed you were. You shouldn't have survived the break, and yet here you are, even with your back to the wall and knife at your throat—"

"What did you just say?" I cut him off.

"You are every bit as strong as—" he began again.

"No, not that part," I cut him off again. The gears were turning inside my mind.

"Even with your back to the wall and a knife to your—"

"Exactly!!!!" I grabbed my boots and tugged them on. Zayne stared at me with questioning eyes, like I had gone *Looney Tunes*, but I shrugged it off.

"I know what we need to do," I said as I finished lacing up my boots. I grabbed my jacket, hat, and gloves. "I need to talk to Juno."

"Juno, as in Junior Black, Juno?" His voice was raised and strained as he said, "Are you crazy?"

"We need more wolves, Zayne. And he can supply them; he didn't lose any people in the massacre because he refused to attend."

"And what makes you think he's going to help us now? We hunted him and his pack down for months, Ezra. We put him in jail. Bash nearly had him charged with your assault!" He was pressing his hand firmly to his temple. I gripped his hands tightly as I looked up at him.

"He has to. If our pack falls, his is next."

"He's a psychopath, I don't trust him," he said, exhaling deeply.

"Neither do I, but I don't have to trust him. I need to use him."

"Okay, fine. But I'm going with you."

"No, I need you to stay here and care for our pack. I don't know if and when Silver Pack will strike, but they'll need you if I haven't returned yet. You're their Beta."

"For the record, I hate this whole plan," he said as he reached out, holding me at arm's length, his hands on my shoulders. "I promised Bash I'd keep you safe, so you better come back, or I'll find you and kick your ass."

"Noted." I laughed as I walked out the door, nearly running over Elder John in the process.

"Oh shit, Elder John, I'm sorry, I didn't mean to," I started, but he hugged me, abruptly halting the apologies spewing from my mouth like word vomit.

"I should have spoken to you sooner. Do you have a moment?" he asked.

"Of course."

"You're smart, Ezra. My son chose well with you, and although I never got to call you my daughter, I know it was his wish to marry you." He cleared his throat and stepped back, holding out a small ornate ring. "This was his mother's when she was Luna. He resized it for you, and I'm sure he'd want you to have it."

"Sir, I…" I was stunned. Bash was going to propose, and…

Tears welled up in my eyes as I took the ring, my hands trembling. "I had no idea," I whispered, feeling the full weight of the ring and of the love it symbolized.

Elder John placed a reassuring hand on my shoulder. "He loved you so deeply, Ezra. And he wanted you to be part of our family. I'm so thankful for the love you showed my son in return. It's comforting that he got a chance to know love before his death."

I nodded, slipping the ring onto my finger. "It wasn't nearly enough time."

"He was my only son." His eyes fell. I didn't know how to comfort him, so I stole a page from Zayne's book and pulled him into my own embrace, as if to shoulder the weight of his words that hit me like a ton of bricks.

"I'm so sorry," I whispered, feeling a lump forming in my throat. "I promise I'll do everything I can to honor him and be worthy of that love."

Elder John nodded, his eyes glistening with unshed tears. "I know you will, Ezra. You're strong, and our pack needs that strength now more than ever, so I want to pledge my support to you. And whatever you've come up with, I would like to accompany you."

"Okay. Then I'll meet you outside in five. We leave as soon as possible."

With a nod, he turned and walked off, leaving me alone in the hall. Staring down at the ring now placed on my finger, the memories of everything we were mixed with the regrets of everything we would never be flooding my mind.

It was beautiful, with *Luna* engraved on the inside of the small ornate band. The band featured a tree filigree with a moonstone at its center. It was every bit befitting of a Luna.

"Mourn later. We have business to attend to."

Lana was right. Scrunching my eyes shut with a force that caused them to ache, I dragged the back of my palms against them, wiping away any and all traces of the tears that threatened to surface again. Then I sucked in a breath and sent Bash all my love with three words I had not yet spoken.

I miss you.

Juno's POV

I had just sat down at the table. The world began to fade away as the dark elixir promising awakening teased my nostrils. The steam revealed the rich, earthy aroma I had been craving. But before that familiar warmth could flood my senses, somebody began banging on my door, causing me to pause. With an irritated grunt, I shot a glance at the watch set on my wrist. 21:20. I set the cup back down and went to the door.

"Hey, Juno, can we come in?" Ezra asked, pushing past me and into the living room of my apartment. Standing in the doorway was none other than Night Tree Pack's previous Alpha, Elder Bingham.

31

"There's something to be said about the company you insist on keeping, my little toy," I said, turning to face the spunky little redhead and pointing to Elder Bingham, who just scoffed as he entered.

"I'm not you're toy, Juno. And I'm here for my pack, so if you could pay attention, this concerns us both," she said, folding her arms against her chest.

"You know, Luna, it's customary to send a request if you have matters to discuss. Not break into another Pack's territory, let alone their Alpha's home."

"I didn't break in. You opened the door."

"Semantics," I said as I the door clicked shut. Heading to the kitchen and pulling the coffee pot off the warmer, I offered, "Coffee?" When they both declined, I returned to the table and finally sipped my cup. *And now it's fucking cold.* If there were two things I absolutely couldn't stand, being told what to do was the first, and cold coffee was a close second.

I pushed it to the center of the table and sat back, "Well, I don't have all night," I said, folding my hands behind my head. "What do you believe concerns us both?"

"Says the guy drinking coffee at nine at night," Ezra sassed back before continuing. "Listen, Gabe's taken about a third of my pack. We lost many in the massacre, and our numbers are thin."

"The point?" I asked, looking over to John. "And why is he even here?"

"I'm here to ensure everything goes smoothly. You don't have to like me, kid, but I'm still an Elder," John said.

"I wasn't aware she needed a bodyguard." I laughed.

"I'm perfectly capable of handling him," Ezra said to John, then turned back to me. "And he's here because I trust him, just as I trust you will do the right thing," she finished.

"And that would be?" I raised my brow.

"Join us," she said as she moved to the table and sat down across from me. "Help us take down Silver Pack."

"I have no qualms with Silver Pack," I said dismissively.

Her icy blue eyes held a glint of mischief, a playful challenge that dared me to meet her gaze as she countered, "Never figured you for someone so incredulous."

"Do not push me, my little toy. I have given you more leniency than most, but I owe you nothing. And first and foremost, I protect what is mine."

"If I may?" John finally spoke.

My irritation was growing. "It's not like any of you Night Tree Pack Members listen anyhow. So, by all means, speak, dog."

Ignoring my words, he asked, "What if you unite the packs?"

Ezra's jaw had fallen, and she stared at John in disbelief. "Ezra," he continued, "you're a Luna without an Alpha, and he's an Alpha without a Luna. You don't need to love him or even like him."

"Good, because I don't," she cut him off.

His eyes softened at her, and he cleared his throat.

"This is about saving both our packs. We need all of us to stand a chance against Silver Pack. So, in order to save our pack, Sebastian's pack, would you marry Junior Black?"

He looked at Ezra, and after a few moments, she said, "Yes, for the sake of the pack."

"And would you take Ezra to be your wife, your Luna, to keep your pack safe? Make no mistake, after he's taken us down, they will come for your pack next."

"No," I answered.

"Are you fucking kidding me?" she asked, staring me down.

"I will, however, take you as my little toy. To have and to play with, in whatever way I see fit."

"You're an asshole," she said with a flip of her middle finger in my direction.

"Better learn to love it, baby."

John cleared his throat. "Well, great! Ezra, you may kiss your husband, and Junior, you may kiss your, uh, little toy."

"What?" Ezra and I both said at the same time.

"I'm ordained, and you both agreed to your union. So kiss, and it will be official."

"Over my dead body," she said through gritted teeth.

"Oh, this is going to be fun." I laughed as I pulled the knife out of the sheath at my side. I reached over the table, grabbed Ezra's hand, yanked it across the table, and held it firmly in place despite her efforts to pull it away.

"Nice ring," I said flatly.

"Fuck off," she spat back.

"Relax, doll," I said as I slid the knife across her palm, slicing through the skin and leaving a trail of blood bubbling to the surface. She flinched, but didn't make a noise. Then I slid the knife across my palm. "It's a blood oath, same as a kiss."

She nodded and allowed me to press her palm to mine.

"Great, so have we just become Storm Cross Pack or Night Tree Pack?" John asked as I ripped a piece of fabric off my white beater and wrapped it around Ezra's hand.

"Thank you," she said, pulling her hand out of my grasp.

I sent her an air kiss and playful wink, which she didn't find amusing. She returned the gesture with narrowed eyes and a sarcastic head bob with her tongue hanging out.

She was clearly not in the mood for my antics, but somehow, getting a rise out of her was entertaining.

"Well?" John asked again.

"Storm Cross," we both said at the same time. The pack name hung in the air between us as we exchanged glances. After years of waiting, the pieces were finally moving into place.

CHAPTER FOUR

Who Said Anything About Wanting Your Heart?

Ezra's POV

"I still can't believe you got married, Ezzie," Kit exclaimed as we moved through the pack house. The once tranquil atmosphere had morphed into one more fit for a mental asylum, with all of Storm Cross's pack members moving in. The chaos around us was overwhelming my senses, and I was on the verge of an emotional collapse.

"Yeah, it all feels…surreal," I replied, dodging a couple of their pack members who were arguing over a piece of furniture. "This is ridiculous. Everything is getting out of hand, and where the fuck is Juno, anyway?"

Kit nodded in agreement, looking around at the bustling scene. "I know, they are a bit extra. Although some of them are growing on me," she finished quickly as she noted another guy who had moved past us, eyeing her up like a piece of candy.

"Gross," I said as we continued.

"What are we talking about?" Zayne asked, coming up from behind us and slinging an arm over each of us, pulling us into his embrace. It still amazes me how close the three of us have become over the last couple of weeks. It felt like this had always been us.

"Oh, Kit here was just saying how…" She gave me a stern look that warned me to keep my mouth shut.

"…this place is becoming a bit out of hand," I finished.

"Have you been to the dining hall yet, Luna?" he asked.

"No?" I asked suspiciously.

"Right, so maybe just try to avoid that part of the pack house, then." He laughed.

Smacking my hands down to my sides with an exasperated sigh, I stopped and turned to look at him. "By the Goddess, Zayne. What could they possibly be doing in the dining hall?" I asked, feeling a mixture of both curiosity and dread.

Zayne smirked. "Let's just say the new recruits decided to have a 'welcome feast,' and things got a bit…out of hand."

I groaned. "Great, just what we need. Guess I'll add that to the list of things to deal with later. Any idea where I can find our new, clearly unbothered Alpha?"

"I have the utmost faith in your abilities to neutralize this mess," Zayne said, giving me a reassuring pat on the back. "And I couldn't tell you, that guy isn't all that warm and welcoming."

"Right," I said as we approached the big wooden door leading into the office. When I opened it, my gaze fell on Junior. I momentarily froze. My fists clenched at my sides, the anger radiating off of me as the heat rose to my cheeks.

"No. Fuck no, get out of his chair!" I yelled as I closed the distance between myself and Juno.

"Calm yourself now, little one. Your fallen lover won't be needing it where he's at."

"Get the FUCK out of the chair, Juno!"

"Lover's quarrel?" asked another man standing off on the side of the room that I hadn't yet noticed.

"And who the fuck are you?" I asked, turning my anger on this new man.

"I like her, Juno. She's definitely spirited." He laughed.

"Spirited. Yes, among other things," Juno replied to the man, but he still didn't bother responding to me.

"Do not fucking push me right now. Your wolves are tearing this place apart, I don't even want to see what happened in the dining hall, and here you are without a care in the goddamn world!"

He didn't move, and I was fuming. I grabbed the letter opener and stabbed it less than an inch from his hand. Finally, he looked up at me, pulled it out of the desk, and tossed it to the side.

"It seems my wife and I have some matters to discuss," he said.

"That's the understatement of the century," I mumbled.

"Beta, please excuse us," he said to the other man.

I looked at the strange man to my right and then glanced behind me at Zayne. No, I've fucking lost so much already. He cannot just come in here and push everyone I care about out.

"He is not our Beta!" I screamed.

"Sure, he is. Alec, meet my Luna. Luna, meet Alec."

"Zayne is our Beta!" I screamed at him, pointing behind me toward Zayne. Who then came forward, putting his arms around my shoulders and turning me to look at him.

"That's not how this works, Ezra. He's our new Alpha and gets to choose his Beta."

"But…"

"It's okay, Ezra. I'll still be by your side if our Alpha accepts my request to be your head Gamma."

Juno looked from me to Zayne and then asked, "It seems she's rather fond of you; should I be worried?"

"Not at all, Alpha. I assure you," he said, bowing his head to Juno, "I only wish to pledge my allegiance to Storm Cross Pack, and I give my word that I will protect our Luna until my last breath."

"Ah," Juno chuckled, "you Night Tree wolves are so formal. If she agrees—"

"I accept," I interrupted and hugged Zayne tightly. "I'm so sorry," I whispered.

"It's really okay. I knew this would happen the second I learned you had married Alpha Black. But I won't break my promise. I will always protect you. I will remain at your side."

"Thank you," I said, releasing him from the embrace.

"Well, great, now that you figured that out, Ezzie. Remember why we came here," Kit said, but she was looking at Zayne. The look on her face…well, I couldn't quite place what it was.

I cleared my throat, turning my attention back to the arrogant fuck in front of me. I'd address that *look* when Kit and I were alone. Right now, there were other issues in need of handling, "Right. Juno—"

"They go. Then we discuss," Juno said, cutting me off.

"For fuck's sake, Juno," I said. The anger flooded back almost instantaneously.

"I stand by my words, little one." He laughed again, and I felt an urge to punch him, to wipe that smug grin right off his face. But I knew that would only give him the satisfaction of seeing me lose control.

"It's fine; I'll go," Kit said, giving me a sympathetic smile. Zayne offered another reassuring squeeze to my shoulder, and then they both left the room. Once they were gone, Juno spoke.

"So, what is it that has your panties in a twist?"

Goddess, this man was infuriating. I took a deep breath, letting the cool air fill my lungs and calm the heat rising within. It did little to calm my racing heart, though, "Other than you still being in that damned chair? How about the lack of organization within this pack? We need structure; your pack is going to destroy this entire pack house!"

"Agreed," he said, much to my surprise. *Was he actually agreeing with me for once?*

"I'll call a formation; you two figure out what you want to do so you can address it," this new Beta, Alec stated.

"Thank you, Alec." Juno waved him off, and then he was gone.

Juno finally moved out of the chair, closing the distance between us by moving around the desk.

"If we have any chance here, you need to trust me, " he said. There was no humor in his tone, no sarcastic bantering, no threatening tones, just a sincere plea that cut through the tension like a knife.

"This alliance was never about trust, Juno; it was about necessity."

Juno's eyes darkened slightly, but he nodded, understanding the gravity of the situation. "Then let's make sure our necessity doesn't turn into regret."

Juno took a deep breath, his resolve hardening. "I get it. We've both got our reasons for joining the packs, but we need to focus on what we can control right now. If you and I aren't on a united front, how do we expect this new pack to be? If we work together, we might have a shot at turning this mess around." He paused and looked at me with a determined glimmer in his eyes. "Let's make this alliance count."

"Is Alec trustworthy?" I asked, taking a step away from him and fiddling with the books on the shelves, busying my fingers to distract myself from the absurd thoughts in my mind.

"He's strong, and he's been my Beta since I took over Storm Cross Pack. I trust him with my very life," he said.

I sighed. I should've expected this. He was an Alpha, and I had only been Luna for a little over a week. Juno was definitely the more experienced of the two of us. I needed his help and guidance, even if that was difficult to admit.

"Thank you for making Zayne my Gamma," I said.

"That was all you, doll. But make no mistakes. You are mine now, and I do not share my toys," he said with a cocky grin.

That arrogance again. What happened to the wise and mature Alpha that had just stood before me?

"You think this is funny?" I spat out, my voice trembling with barely contained rage. "Do you really think you can just laugh everything off?"

Juno's eyes twinkled with a mix of amusement and something darker. *Malice? Anger?* No. That wasn't it. *Have I always been this bad at reading people?*

"Oh, but it is amusing, my little one. Watching you struggle, watching you fight against the inevitable. It's all a game, and you're playing your part perfectly."

My fists clenched against my sides, my nails digging into my palms, drawing a thin line of blood. "This isn't a game, Juno. Not to me. Not to our pack members. People could get hurt; people could die!"

His laughter faded, replaced by a cold, calculating stare that had me frozen in place yet again. "Then perhaps it's time you learned the rules, little toy. Because in this game, there are no winners. Only survivors."

"I may be your Luna, but we both know I will never be yours. I will never be your *little toy*," I hissed back at him.

"You will."

"I won't. I already gave my heart away, and it shattered with him."

"Oh, little one, who said anything about wanting your heart?" he asked, stepping closer and pinning me between his body and the bookcase behind me. The shelves were digging into my back, causing a sharp pain to run down my spine. His breath was warm against my ear as he whispered, "All I want from you is your loyalty and…" he paused, "your obedience. Only then can we rebuild what is broken."

I swallowed hard, trying to ignore how his proximity quickened my pulse. "Loyalty and obedience?" I asked, my voice barely above a whisper.

He nodded, his eyes locking on mine. His eyes weren't brown like Bash's or green like Gabe's; they held a glimmer of both—a beautiful, powerful, and violent maelstrom of the two.

"That's all I need, my little toy. We both have our scars, but we can forge something stronger together. Something unbreakable."

"Great. Now, can you move? Back. Now," I said, my voice steadying, enunciating every word with a cold, commanding edge. And he did, with that same cocky grin he wore the first day I had met him in the alley.

"I'll give you my loyalty, but do not expect my blind obedience. Only I command my actions. And my heart…it remains my own." I turned and went to Bash's chair. "This chair will be moved to my room after we leave here. Is that understood?" I asked.

"What is it with you and this chair?" he asked.

I remembered the way Bash had taken me in this chair. The way he completely fell apart for me until the only thing left was our primal need for one another, nothing but the love we had for each other coursing through our veins.

That was the last time I had Bash entirely to myself. He promised he would stand by my side forever, that it was not the end for us, and that he would give me his love forever. *He lied.*

Neither of us could control the future, but I would love him until I breathed my last dying breath. Seeing Juno in this chair infuriated me beyond belief. This was my memory. One I would cherish until I one day joined my mate in the unknown.

"It's all I have left of him," I said, the tears gathering again, but this time I didn't hold them back. I cried for him, I mourned for him, I fell apart for him. The same soul-crushing way he had fallen apart for me that day. I didn't care that Juno was here; I didn't care about anything at all except the all-consuming emptiness in my heart that Bash's death had left me with.

"Cry for him, mourn his loss, this once. Then, pick yourself up and forget it. This weakness will kill us all," he said, turning and leaving, the door falling shut behind him as my cries echoed through the night, a haunting reminder of the desolation that had taken hold by the loss of my other half. Leaving me with this deep, aching void that nothing and no one could ever fill.

Zayne came rushing in, but he didn't ask questions, for the longest time he didn't say a word. He simply held me as I cried.

"Don't listen to him, Ezzie. You saved us all, and it's okay to miss him. I miss him, too. I'm so sorry; you should never have had to deal with any of this; this is all my fault."

"I…I *need* him," I cried. "I can't do this without him."

"Yes, you can, Ezzie. Cause he's still here." He pushed his hand against my chest where my heart should be. But he was wrong; I felt my heart rip straight from my chest when he died. There was nothing left there, only emptiness.

"I can't feel him anymore, Zayne. And I hate it. It's like I lost the best part of me."

"I know." Zayne's face fell before he continued speaking. "All he wanted was for you to be safe and alive. Mating, the bond, you being Luna, I forced that on both of you. I will never be able to make up for that, but I will always stand with you, Ez. I will spend my life trying to make up for all of it. All you need to do is live. If you can't do it for you, then do it for him. Because if you give up, his death will have been for nothing."

He was mostly wrong; he shouldn't have any guilt about pushing me and Bash to mate. That was one regret I didn't have.

The one thing he was right about, however. Even if I didn't want to live without Bash, I knew that what he wanted most was for me to go on without him. I just never knew how hard it would be to do that for him. I still didn't understand why he had to go, why any of this had to happen, why the Moon Goddess had taken him from me just as swiftly as she brought him to me. We didn't even get one year together, in that, lies my regrets.

"None of this is your fault, Zayne. I am so happy that I got the short time I did with Bash. I hate myself most. I denied the bond for so long; I missed out on so much time with him and so much love. If I had just accepted it, Gabe never would have happened. It's my guilt, my burden to bear, not yours," I said, reaching out, taking his hands in mine and giving them a gentle squeeze. "Seriously, thank you for the push."

"Anytime," he responded, the ghost of a smile spreading along his jawline. Although his eyes couldn't lie, they told me he still blamed himself. I was his burden, just as Gabe was mine. We were undeniably entangled in the aftermath of losing Bash. And I was thankful that Bash had brought us together. Maybe he knew we would need to borrow each other's strength to push forward.

"Okay," I said, wiping the remnants of all the tears from my face. "We will keep fighting, keep living, for Bash. Can you...?"

"Alpha Black already asked me to take the chair to your room."

"He did?" How uncharacteristically kind of him.

"Yes, now get cleaned up. Unless you aren't feeling up to it, you have a battle assembly to attend," Zayne said, standing and pulling me up with him. "It's okay if you need more time."

"I should be there for our pack," I said, but before I turned to leave, I looked at Zayne. "Thank you."

"Always, my Luna," he said, grabbing the chair and wheeling it down the hall behind me, every squeak and squeal of the wheels echoing as I raised my head and made my way to Bash's bedroom. Sending up my solemn vow to my mate.

I will be stronger for you, Bash.

CHAPTER FIVE

Careful, Dolly.

Ezra's POV

"Your Luna wished to be here, but it seems she was not feeling…"

When I entered, the battle assembly was in formation. The heavy doors clanged shut behind me, echoing through the stillness as Juno's words halted. The sound reverberated as I strolled in as if it was announcing my presence with a weighty significance.

As I made my way to the stage, I took in the sight before me, which I admit made me feel at ease. But it was also surprising considering the shit storm Juno's pack brought with it…I mean, how the fuck did Alec manage to organize a formation like this when the last few days have been such a disaster?

The Gammas and Warriors were broken into sections near the front, and towards the back were lines of wolves who had agreed to fight despite not being warriors. They would need some in-depth training before we attacked, which was evident by the lack of precision and uniformity in their stances. Sadly, I also fit into this category.

But I held my head high as I continued marching forward. Junior and Alec stood at the podium in front. "Your Luna is feeling just fine," I stated as I took my place next to Junior. "And I apologize for my tardiness, as I had important issues to deal with."

Junior's mouth twisted into a mischievous grin as he looked down at me, which I returned with an eye roll. Then he lifted the microphone back to his lips and continued speaking.

"Alright, recruits, listen up! I know things have been chaotic since the joining of our packs. That ends today! We're here to establish a new order. The joining of our packs marks a new era, one where unity and solidarity will be our greatest weapons. I don't care if you were born a child of Storm Cross or a child of Night Tree. Time is not a luxury that we have, so from this moment forward, know that we are one! War is coming, and we must join together in this fight!"

He handed the mic to me, and I looked at him nervously. Great, another speech. This time, with twice as many people.

"Just speak the truth," he whispered in my ear as he took a step back. I looked from him to the recruits before me, then swallowed either the sickening effect he had on me or my pride. Both left a bitter taste in my mouth at this point, so I couldn't tell you which it was.

I held my hand out to him, and he chuckled as he took it, allowing me to pull him to my side. "We will stand together, stronger than ever. Every one of you is crucial in the upcoming battle. We train, we fight, we bleed as one! Remember why we're fighting. This isn't just about territory, but about our future as a pack. We fight now to ensure our family's safety! We fight for our honor! We fight for our freedom! They murdered Night Tree's Alpha and plunged us into the depths of despair, but we will emerge from the shadows. United."

The crowd grew loud, chanting, "WE TRAIN, WE FIGHT, WE BLEED AS ONE!" as I returned the microphone to Junior. He looked annoyed at my bringing up Bash, which left me feeling more than a little satisfied. After a few more chants, he held his hand up in a fist, which quieted the recruits.

"When the time comes, we'll face the Silver Pack head-on, with courage and determination. Gabriel Knight is not going to take our land or our freedom! Let's show them what we're made of! We have a lot of training to do, and teamwork is vital to success. What is Storm Cross pack going to do?!"

He paused, and the chant rang out again loud and in unison.

"WE TRAIN, WE FIGHT, WE BLEED AS ONE!"

"That's right! Your commanding officers have already been briefed on the battle strategies. So, rest tonight, brothers and sisters, for tomorrow, we train!"

I was in awe of Junior and of myself. *Who knew we could command such power and respect?* Of course, there was a lot I didn't know about this man—not that I intended to get to know him. He was a means to an end. Our marriage was only a tool, a necessity of war.

Once the recruits were dismissed, he pulled me to the side. "I've ordered some scouts out to Silver Pack's borders to see if they can gather any helpful information. We need to know their strengths and any weaknesses they might have. Are you ready for this?" he asked, staring at me again like he was searching for something.

"What?" I snapped.

"Have you handled it? Your weakness? We can't afford for you to break down once the battle begins."

I flipped him off, irritated at the accusation that I couldn't keep my shit together, despite the evidence being in his favor.

"Maybe later," he said with a smirk before walking off.

Fucking asshole.

"As if that would ever happen!" I yelled after him, but it didn't matter. He was already out the door.

After everyone cleared out, I set up a temporary office in the dining room. The displacement I had felt since Junior and his heathens moved in here had me reeling, but for now, I'd make do.

Trying to think of weaknesses that might help us was pointless. Gabe had no heart or soul. The only weakness we currently had working in our favor was the wound I left in his stomach. But I knew that the longer we waited, the more healed he would be, and soon, even that wouldn't help us.

For right now, I could only hope it kept him from attacking long enough for some of our non-warriors to learn how to protect themselves—so, moving on. I collected all the blueprints currently at our disposal, looking over them in great detail.

First, I looked over our estate. It was large. Towering trees cloaked the land in perpetual twilight, with a long road winding up the hill where the manor stood proud and timeless, its stone walls whispering tales of past generations. But it wasn't gated. Making the woods and the multitude of paths that wound through lush gardens vulnerable.

Although I admit, the paths where moonflowers would bloom under the watchful eye of the night sky were beautiful.

Time had gotten away from me as I looked over Silver Pack's compound, and when the big clock at the end of the dining hall chimed, my heart nearly jumped from my chest.

Was it already midnight?

I began gathering the documents and cleaning up the plates from my dinner, reviewing the data and facts I had learned. That compound was located centrally, outside of Oakland, in a gated community.

In order to get to Gabe, we would need to reach the main pack house. Scaling the gates, which stood approximately ten feet tall, based on the blueprints, wouldn't be easy. Any larger weaponry was out of the question. Other than our wolves, we'd be limited to compact weapons. Handguns and knives. Then, there was about a mile of pack homes between the gate and the pack house, making any sneak attack nearly impossible.

We didn't stand a chance with any large-scale attack, either; he'd be alerted long before we got anywhere close to him. So, what did all of this information tell me? On the defensive, we were sitting ducks. On the offensive, we were even more fucked. Gabe's pack house might as well be the western penitentiary and Gabe the warden. Nobody was getting in or out without his say-so.

I couldn't contain myself. Right now, it felt like we had already lost the war. Literally and metaphorically screwed on every front. I swept my arm across the table, knocking everything to the floor as I let out the frustration that had been building all night. A loud shrieking yell escaped from the depths of my soul.

His voice behind me scared the shit out of me, my body mimicking the jolt I felt in my chest when he spoke.

"Stop making a mess."

"What the fuck do you want?" I asked as I knelt down to gather up the blueprints scattered across the floor.

"You're acting like a child, " Junior said, moving around the table until he towered over me. "You know, under different circumstances, this view might be enjoyable." He chuckled.

"What the fuck is wrong with you?" I asked as I stood up.

"So much, little doll," he said, taking the maps from my arms and setting them down on the table. "And you should be resting."

"I'll rest when this is over."

"You'll rest now; you've got training in the morning. That isn't a request."

"We're fucked," I said, sitting on the table, leaning my elbows onto my knees, and cradling my face as I looked over at him.

"What happened to that determined young woman who barged into my apartment last week? I need her. I need that fire I saw that night, not…whatever the fuck this is. What are you thinking?" he asked, sitting down at the table across from me. He was the last person I wanted to talk to right now, but we were…

What even were we?

Husband and wife? I had to choke down the bile rising in my throat when I thought about that. Nope. *Partners?* But that didn't seem right either. *Aligned?* That was maybe the most fitting description. We were aligned, much to my dismay, and if I needed to talk to anyone right now, it was him.

"We can't attack straight on," I said.

"Nope, we'd get our asses handed to us. What else?"

"Our pack house isn't built for a defensive stance; sure, the hill gives us a slight advantage, but we're defenseless. They can walk right in."

"So, what does that leave us with?"

"Middle ground, or…"

"Or what, my little toy? I see those gears moving."

"I'm not your toy; first off," I gave him a stern middle finger, "and second, we need to fortify the pack house."

"Once the scouts return, we'll know what we're fighting against. Then we will know what actions to take."

He had already thought about all of this. *Asshole.*

"Why didn't you tell me you had already come to this conclusion?" I asked, moving forward.

"Maybe I like watching you squirm?" he asked, raising his brow at me.

"I fucking hate you."

He smiled as he stood up, scooping me in his arms like a small child.

"Put me the fuck down, Junior. Put me down NOW!" I screamed as I began kicking my legs, punching his chest, trying to get out of his grasp. He did eventually let go of my legs so that I was standing, but kept me locked in his grasp.

"We might be married, but you are absolutely nothing more than a means to an end," I spat at him.

"Wrong. I told you. You're mine."

"I am not yours," I scoffed.

"You *are* mine."

"I'll kill you before I ever let you touch me," I said, disgusted by the sight of him and his words.

He pulled out a knife, pressing it firmly to my neck. "You aren't scaring anyone," he said, pulling my body into him. "And if I want you, then I will have you."

I wrapped my hand around his, pressing the knife harder into the soft tissue of my neck; I felt the familiar burn as the knife broke through skin, a satisfying trickle of blood soon following. I leaned up and whispered into his ear, "I told you once already, didn't I? If you're gonna cut me, then fucking cut me."

"You know I will have the taste of your blood in my mouth…" he promised as he pressed the blade between my legs. "Careful, dolly."

"I *hate* you," I repeated as he leaned into me. I could feel the table curving under my ass as I struggled to stay upright. I tried to brace myself against it, but he pushed me back. I fell forcefully onto the table as he grabbed a fist full of my hair, pulling my face to his with the knife still placed firmly between my thighs.

"Junior, STOP!"

I couldn't say why…but suddenly, this no longer felt like a game I wanted to play. He was serious, and for the first time since I had met him, I was feeling something besides annoyance towards this man. For the first time, I was genuinely afraid of what he might do.

"I said STOP!!!" I screamed as I pushed back against his chest. Only to realize that it was utterly pointless.

I mean, this man was tall. I'm not sure how tall. But I'd say well over six feet. He had a surprisingly muscular build. Normally, he wore loose fitting clothing so, if I hadn't felt them—if I hadn't pushed against his hardened chest, I'd have never guessed he was built like a brick house under his clothes.

But he was. He had broad shoulders that gave way to perfectly sculpted biceps. The intricacies of his build were well-defined by muscles. His narrow waist only accentuated the massive definition of his upper body. He didn't need any of that when his aura seemed to intimidate those around him without putting his aesthetically pleasing physique on display.

But it was clear that he had spent years sculpting it. If he had any scars, I'm sure he'd wear them like a badge of honor. His eyes, piercing and resolute when he looked at me, reflected the depths of his dubious intent. I knew I wasn't in control, and his words only confirmed what my desperation already knew.

"It doesn't matter how much you plead, little one. Do you really think anything you say or do will stop me from taking you right here and right now if that's what I want?"

It's true, I had no chance of stopping him. Still, that didn't mean I needed to make this pleasant for him. I spat in his face.

"That won't be happening," he said as he cut the crotch of my jeans with one fluid motion…pressing his hand down on my throat. His touch was firm and possessive, and I was devoid of air. As I struggled to find my next breath, the world around us began to spot, and tiny bursts of light sparked along the corners of my vision.

It felt like I was slipping away into a new world—a world where I no longer existed. Or maybe just another time, a time when Bash hadn't been taken from me, and this war didn't exist. One where in its place, light and darkness intertwined in a beautiful dance of both passion and despair.

He was positioning himself between my thighs, dropping the knife to the side to guide his now exposed cock into my entrance. I was weak, too weak to stop it.

As he thrust into me, I gasped—still semi-aware of the horrors that were happening in the real world. But it was like the signals were misfiring in my brain. At this point, I couldn't decipher between what was real and what was a dream. Somehow, in this transient state, the indisputable truth that Bash was gone didn't seem to register.

But was this really happening at all?

I tried to fight against his hand on my throat, against his body between my legs, against his cock moving inside me. But I was powerless against him, and he continued thrusting hard and deep.

"If you don't like it, why are you so wet, dolly?"

I couldn't answer him. I knew that I didn't want him to touch me, but my body was responding in ways it shouldn't have been. It was wrong—I knew it was wrong. I hated him, but even so, my body had been craving this sensation. The ache, the pain, the pleasure he was giving me, it emptied my mind.

A moan escaped my lips, and his grip loosened slightly, a knowing smirk spreading across his face.

"Don't." I breathed…

"Don't what, doll…?"

"Don't go easy on me now."

I looked up at him, begging for it, pleading with him silently. I didn't want to think. I didn't want to remember. I didn't want to mourn *him* anymore.

Junior's hand tightened against my throat as he gave me the most savage, most profound pounding I had ever had.

"You like it, don't you, dolly? Say it," he commanded as he released my throat, but I didn't. I didn't say anything. He reached down, gripping my hips and thrusting harder still, forcing in every inch again and again until I felt that familiar warmth and tension spreading through my body.

My muscles tightened with anticipation, and my heartbeat raced frantically in my chest, each beat echoing the mounting pleasure. It felt like this was something I had been waiting for, something I wanted or maybe needed to feel.

The tingling sensation, deeply rooted within my abdomen, which was being brutally assaulted by Juno's massive size, began radiating outward, all-encompassing, as it pulled me toward the most Earth-shattering orgasm I had ever experienced.

I can't explain the sounds that vibrated in my chest, escaping from my mouth. Or the way my body shook uncontrollably while my hands were white knuckled on the end of the table. Maybe that was my attempt to bring me back to Earth. Until he came inside my beaten, raw, and probably bruised body, leaving me breathless.

I hurt in ways I'd never known. The euphoric orgasm dulled all the hate and anger I felt for this man temporarily as I struggled to wrap my mind around what had just happened.

Time had slowed, all my worries had dissolved, and all that remained was an overwhelming sense of peace and contentment.

But that can't be right, can it?

He just took me despite my pleas not to. So then, why did it feel like I was dancing with the stars, where every step was light and every movement effortless? I stared up at him in shock, anger, disgust, and…complete and utter confusion.

"You're welcome," he said as he rearranged himself, zipping up his jeans and stepping away from me.

I sat up. "For what? For raping me? You're fucking insane."

"Deny it all you want, my little toy. But you *are* mine. And you will know it. It doesn't matter where. It doesn't matter when. If I want you, then I will have you."

"No. This was wrong, and it will never happen again, you hear me?!"

The tears began to fall like glistening pearls, carving delicate paths down my cheeks now that the sexual high was gone. I couldn't make a sound, as the shimmer of liquid sorrow fell.

They caught the light and refracted before falling away, vanishing into the ether. Tracing the contours of my face was a clear and visible sign of my vulnerability, a testament to the pain inflicted, and I wondered if my silent cries echoed through the chambers of his conscience in the slightest as he looked at me.

"Can you walk?" he asked.

"I'm fine," I sniffled as I tried to get to my feet, but my legs buckled. Had his arms not been there, I'm sure I would have fallen. I gave him what I'm sure was the look of death as he quickly picked me up.

"Relax, I'm just taking you to bed."

But why? After what you had just done, why take me to bed?

My throat was feeling the effects of his hold now, and my voice was strained as I reasserted, yet again, "I hate you."

I expected a chuckle. But it never came.

"Good," he said flatly as he started walking from the dining hall with me in his arms.

"I'll never forgive you for this." My voice was barely a whisper, hoarse and trembling. Each word was slow and labored, my breath shallow, punctuated by pauses as I struggled to find the strength to keep my eyes open.

I was spent, but when he spoke again, my eyes opened enough to meet his gaze and caught the ambiance of a lingering darkness there.

"I didn't say I deserved your forgiveness…but also, I wasn't asking for it."

"Good. Because you'll never have it," I said in the same labored response, my head falling involuntarily into his chest.

"Shhh. Plenty of time to hate me tomorrow," he whispered as I felt him place a small kiss on my forehead. I was way too exhausted to fight him. But I did wipe it off with the back of my palm. Which just made him chuckle. It wasn't long before he slid me into my bed.

"Goodnight, my Luna."

Not little toy?

Not dolly?

Not little one?

My Luna.

Goddess, this man is a mindfuck.

CHAPTER SIX

When Does This Get Easier?

Ezra's POV

I don't remember falling asleep that night. But I remember thinking about what it felt like to be trapped under Junior. I remember his weight bearing down on me in a way that left me completely helpless.

I could still feel the phantom pain of his hand around my neck and the way the world around me seemed to fade away under the pressure of it. I remember being stupid enough to provoke him in the first place. Not knowing he was capable of such a thing. But it's hard to know what people keep buried beneath the surface.

That's a lesson I should have already learned, but was stupid enough to repeat. Maybe because I had told myself for so damn long to forget it, perhaps I had tricked my mind into believing it never happened, or at least, I had buried it far enough in the back of my mind, I had almost forgotten it. But we never truly forget, do we? The bad things.

Like Mom, the good memories you want to hold onto always seem to fade over time. Sometimes, I can barely remember her face. But those bad ones somehow always revisit us, don't they? This one always seemed to come back, eventually.

I thought escaping Dad would leave it buried this time, with every other secret. Never to be spoken out loud. *How naïve.*

***

Knock, knock, knock.

I closed my eyes tightly, pulling the covers over my head. Maybe if he thought I was asleep, he'd go away.

"Ezraaaa, are youu awake?" His slurred words cut through the wooden door, taking hold of my mind as the subtle rattle of the doorknob filled the air with dread, a tentative twist that quickly turned into a more forceful jiggling.

No. I'm not.

It grew quiet, apart from the light shuffling of his feet against the hardwood floor as he walked away. But it wasn't long before the metal components began to click and clatter again, as another attempt to open the door was made. A faint key scraped against the lock, a metallic whisper of frustration, before it slowly creaked open. The sound sent a shiver down my spine.

His hand on my hip had startled me, and I knew I had made a mistake when I gasped. Still, I refused to open my eyes.

He and Mom had been fighting again, which meant she was most likely sleeping somewhere in the house.

Mom always said to hide. "Plug your ears, my little love, and sing our favorite song, okay? Whatever you do, stay in your room."

But sometimes, being in my room didn't save me. Sometimes, waking up from her naps took Mom a long time. And Dad had a favorite way to pass the time. One I didn't much like.

"I know you're awake; don't make this hard on Daddy. Or next time, Momma won't wake up. Our little secret. Remember?"

"Don't hurt my Mommy!" I cried softly into my pillow.

"Come here, Ezra. If you're a good girl, Mommy will be fine."

"Don't touch me!" I yelled as his hand shifted, lifting my shirt. I tried to run away. But he grabbed me by my hair, yanking me back to the bed. His hand was abruptly on the back of my neck as he pushed my face down into the mattress, muffling my screams. His other hand, under my belly, lifting me so that he could...

***

The loud knocking on the bedroom door woke me the following day. It pulled me from my worst childhood memory, saving me from reliving that violent molestation.

Sweat-soaked sheets and a still-racing heart reminded me of the day I learned what no eight-year-old child should.

Sometimes, the world is unkind, and people aren't what they seem. Sometimes fathers don't love and protect their children, but instead, break them in the worst ways imaginable.

Sometimes, moms leave, and we never know why. We blame ourselves. Because we're beaten every day and told it was our fault. We weren't a *good girl*, and that's the last memory you get of your mother.

Her once gentle eyes blazed with a fire of protectiveness and despair, reflecting the shock and searing pain of the moment. I had believed her reassuring promises that it was all going to be okay before she left me to suffer alone. *A damn liar.* That's all she was.

I glanced at the alarm clock on the stand beside the bed: 3:45 a.m. *Today was going to be hell.* I pulled the blankets back over my head and rolled over. Pushing the memory aside, trying to remember and forget my mother's face. I have a different demon to focus on today, at 4:00 am. Training. Another form of torture courtesy of our new Alpha.

Zayne's voice was quiet as the bedroom door creaked open. "Ezra?"

"Yeah, I know. I'm coming," I said as I sat up in bed, flopping the covers off to the side.

Zayne's usual playful grin washed out the instant he saw me. His face paled as his eyebrows began to knit together in concern, and he approached me slowly like he was unsure if his eyes were playing tricks on him.

That shift in Zayne suddenly had me looking down at myself in horror. I was wearing my favorite sleep shorts and a silk button-down pajama top. I don't remember changing, but I chose to ignore that fact. I looked over my body, and nothing seemed out of sorts. I questioned him, confused and slightly disturbed by the look on his face.

"What?"

"Ezra, what happened?" he probed, his voice a mix of worry and bewilderment.

My lack of response seemed to irritate him further because the softness had vanished entirely from his voice as he moved closer. "Who fucking hurt you, Ezra?"

"Who hurt me?" I asked, and then he was in front of me.

"Your neck, Ezra. It's…" His hands moved to his throat, and instinctively, I mirrored his movements.

Oh shit. My eyes widened as I felt the sharp reminder of the pain. My throat was tender and sore, warm to the touch, and throbbing like I could feel my heartbeat pulsing through it. I quickly pulled my collar up over the marks I knew must be present on my neck. "It's nothing,

Zayne. Just…an accident," I stammered, avoiding his gaze as I jumped up, running to the bathroom vanity.

Sure enough, there was a fresh, reddish handprint that wrapped around my throat. Juno's handprint, which was sporting a thin red line where the knife had pierced my skin. *How could I not know?* Maybe I had been blocking out the pain, but I felt like an idiot.

Zayne followed me into the bathroom. "An accident?" he repeated. "That doesn't look like a fucking accident to me, Ezra. How the fuck did that happen?"

My mind was racing. It was a simple truth. So why was I suddenly feeling like that same stupid girl I used to be, ready to talk through her ass to explain it all away? Unsure of how to respond, I bit my lip. The memories of the night before came flooding back. The intense, confusing mix of emotions—anger, pleasure, regret—swirled within me.

He raped me. But technically, he's my husband, my Alpha. Is it really rape if we're already married? Heat rose in my core as I remembered how aggressively he took me.

"Zayne, please just drop it," I pleaded, my voice barely above a whisper. "It's complicated."

"Complicated?" Zayne echoed, his frustration evident as he continued. "Ezra, I'm your friend, your Gamma. I'm supposed to protect you. Tell me who it was, and I promise I'll take care of it. Whoever hurt you is a traitor to our pack and will be punished accordingly."

I sighed; I wanted to tell him everything, to unload the tangled mess of feelings I was currently struggling with, but I couldn't. Maybe it was the fear of judgment that was holding me back.

"I appreciate it, Zayne, really. But this particular situation isn't one you can correct. I'll have to figure this one out on my own." My voice wavered, and Zayne hesitated, clearly torn. I knew he wanted to protect me, but finally, he nodded. The worry in his eyes remained as he spoke. "Ezra? You know, you're not alone. Not anymore."

"Zayne, I'm really okay, but I'm gonna need a minute to get ready," I said, fumbling through the drawers, searching desperately for anything to cover this up. I had some makeup here, but Bash…

Bash.

Oh, my Goddess. Why does it feel like I just cheated on him? And what's worse, I might have even enjoyed it. That realization came with even more fucking tears. *When does this get easier?* I lost my breath. Snot was bubbling out of my nose, and I was hysterical at this point, unable to keep my knees steady. Zayne's arms wrapped around me and pulled me into his chest.

"Zayne," I cried out his name; it was all I could manage before falling victim to the guilt, shame, and pain coursing through my mind and dropping to the floor in his arms.

"Shhh, it's okay. It's okay. I've got you." He hushed and soothed me, rubbing his hand over my head. It was so comforting, so easy to fall apart with him. Eventually, my breath began to level out again. He pulled out his phone and quickly texted over my shoulder before pocketing it again.

"You're okay. Everything is gonna be okay," he continued.

His voice was like a balm, soothing the frayed edges of my nerves. I leaned into his touch. The world outside blurred, leaving just the two of us in this cocoon of calm. His presence was a gentle anchor, holding me steady while my internal storm began to subside. I didn't realize how tightly I had been holding onto him, clinging to the warmth of his body until he spoke.

His words were a soft murmur in my ear, grounding me further. "I will always be here," he whispered, his breath warm against my skin. I felt another tear escape, but this time it wasn't from sadness, but from the overwhelming relief of no longer having to carry all the weight by myself.

"But Ezra…I can't breathe." He laughed. "You're squeezing the life out of me. It's too tight."

I exhaled sharply; snot was running down my face now, and I loosened my grip on him.

"Oh Goddess, I'm so sorry, Zayne." I laughed and cried as Kit came running into the bathroom. He smiled at me and then at her. "I just thought maybe you needed a friend."

"I did. Lucky me, now I have two," I said, pulling Kit into our tangled mess on the bathroom floor. Kit lost her footing, falling and rolling to the side. Zayne was there before I could react, catching her before she hit the floor. Their eyes met, and I watched Kit's cheeks flush red before she glanced away, flustered.

Zayne's eyes softened with concern. "Are you okay?" he asked gently, still holding her steady.

Kit nodded, her voice barely above a whisper, "Yeah, thanks."

Silence fell over the three of us.

"Well, it looks like I'm not the only one who needed a friend today." My voice was light and teasing as I stood up. A knowing smile played on my lips as I watched the two of them. "You two look pretty cozy down there."

Kit immediately shot me *the look* and moved off Zayne's lap as he cleared his throat.

"Would you two like some alone time?" I laughed as I wiped my nose, grabbed the compact from the vanity, and began my best attempt at covering the red patches on my throat.

"Oh no, you don't," Kit said, grabbing my wrist and forcing me to look at her. "I'm not Zayne, and I'm not gonna let you bullshit your way out of this. Tell me what the fuck happened."

"It's nothing, Kit. I'm really okay."

Kit turned to Zayne, and he seemed to get the point. These two were freakishly *on the same wavelength.* He patted both our shoulders as he moved out of the bathroom. When he exited the room, Kit grabbed the compact out of my hands. "First off, you should be better at this by now," she said, setting it down and pulling the color corrector and concealer out of her bag. "I would've been here faster, but…camouflage."

She began applying the color corrector and then, as she picked up the concealer, looked me dead in the eyes and said, "Talk, Ezzie."

Great. How do I tell *Momma Kit* I told him not to touch me, but maybe I'm glad he didn't listen. He hurt me, but I'm seriously so fucked up that I'm pretty sure I liked it. It was just sex. And just so happened to be precisely what I needed, with everything else going on. But also, I feel all this guilt and fucking pain for dishonoring Bash in this way. I was deep in thought when Kit snapped me out of it.

"I knew it," she said as she applied the concealer. "I don't care if he is our new Alpha; he's dead."

"I didn't even say anything, Kit!"

"You didn't have to, Ezzie. I know you better than you do. And your face told me everything I needed to know. Besides, it's hard to miss the way he looks at you. It's so intense. I can't get it out of my mind. There's something very off about that guy," she said as she finished off with the compact powder.

As she faced me toward the mirror, I couldn't believe it. The mark was completely gone.

"Holy shit!" I exclaimed.

"I know, I'm a freaking rockstar," she said.

"Kit," I looked over my shoulder at her, "it's more complicated than you think; Juno may have left those marks, but—and I'm hoping for zero judgment here—I think I needed it. The sex was..."

"Hold up, sex? You had sex with him?" She seemed surprised, but as she inhaled a deep breath, her eyes softened. "Hey, no judgment here."

She placed a comforting hand on my shoulder. "We all have our reasons for the things that we do. Just…make sure you're taking care of yourself, okay? I don't trust him, and it's only been a few weeks since…"

"Bash, yeah, I know. And I feel like shit. It's not like I forgot about him. I can't get him out of my head. It's like every little thing reminds me of him, and then it hurts all over again. I honestly don't even know; the sex just happened, but for the first time since The Silver Moon, I didn't feel sad; I just felt..."

"His hand around your throat?" she asked, raising a brow.

"Shut up. I was gonna say I just felt good. For once, I wasn't thinking about him and missing him, but now? I feel awful."

"Ezzie, no one is expecting you to get over him; you lost your mate. That's something very few wolves even live through. You've been putting on that brave face, but I can see how badly you're hurting. And that's okay."

"I know, but it hurts so bad all the time," I said softly.

Kit nodded, her eyes glistening with understanding. "Well, I think he'd want you to be happy, no matter how, and I think he'd understand that you're just trying to find your way through this. It's okay to feel lost sometimes."

"Thanks, Kit."

"4:15!" Zayne yelled into the room. "I'm not rushing you ladies, but we are going to be really late for battle training, so if you could wrap it up for now, that would be great."

Kit and I exchanged amused glances. "Did you know he was gonna stay out there?" I asked, laughing.

Kit shook her head, grinning. "Nope, but you know Zayne, as your head Gamma and protector, I doubt he'll ever leave your side now."

"Goddess, I hope you're wrong; that could make the sex a little awkward," I mused.

Kit made a vomiting gesture into her mouth, and then we both burst into laughter. I snorted and added. "I couldn't tell him what happened, Kit. Bash was his best friend, his brother…I mean, I didn't plan for it to happen, I told him to stop, but…"

Kit's laughter stopped, and she cut me off. "He…raped you, Ezzie?"

"He's my husband, Kit," I said, shaking my head.

"Doesn't matter, Ezzie. We all know this wasn't a marriage of love; he has no right to force you to…what was his goal? That guy is…"

"I don't know, Kit. I need to talk to him."

"If you didn't want him to touch you, and he didn't listen, that's rape, Ezzie."

"But what if I didn't want it, but needed it? What if he somehow knew that I needed it?"

Kit didn't say anything. Goddess, this was all so confusing. I didn't even know how to feel.

"Please, just let me figure this out on my own."

"I don't like him," Kit assured me.

"I don't either, in fact. I hate that arrogant fuck."

Kit choked out a laugh, "Well, at least I know you haven't been brainwashed. Just know, if he hurts you, being Alpha won't save him. Not from Zayne. And certainly not from me."

"I know, Kit; I love you."

"Love you, too, babes. But seriously, we should get moving," she pulled me into a quick hug and kissed my forehead, "before Zayne decides to write us up for *excessive dawdling*."

When we exited the bedroom, Zayne flashed us that mischievous grin and said, "Took you long enough! I was beginning to think you'd forgotten we were heading to battle training. But hey, at least you'll be the best-looking warriors out there!" He shot me and Kit a wink. "You look great, Ezra."

"Thanks, Kit's truly gifted in the art of makeup." I laughed.

"Not that she needs it," he said, sending a smile her way that made her blush even brighter. And just like that, I found my smile again. Just in time to enter battle training.

CHAPTER SEVEN

Breaking You Was the Promise

Juno's POV

The sun still hung low in the sky, casting long shadows across the training grounds. Last night, a light dusting of snow fell, and the chilled air had me crossing my arms tightly over my chest as I scanned the grounds, my eyes sharp as they followed the trainees' movements. Today's drills were simple and designed to assess each recruit's individual skills.

When I saw Ezra enter the training grounds, Zayne and Kit were beside her. I cast a fleeting look at my watch—twenty-six minutes past four. A scoff escaped my lips, a mixture of surprise and irony that she had deigned to arrive at all. Part of me didn't expect to see her here after last night, but there she was. The other part of me was impressed that despite what I did to her, her face still lit up the world around her.

As I followed her movements, my mind wandered, wondering what things would have been like had her mother succeeded all those years ago in leaving her father. I thought about the things her father had done to her and to the life she must have suffered through at the hands of Thorin, *the bastard.* My hands were curling into fists involuntarily at my sides.

I remembered that shy but beautiful little girl who had been promised to me, and I couldn't help but wonder if she would still be the same girl standing before me now if she had escaped him.

I had only seen her that one time; something about those red curls and those blue eyes had cast its wicked spell on my heart.

I had waited in the shadows for them to return to me that night like Lina had promised.

No one came.

A week after that meeting, I received correspondence from Lina. She said leaving was too dangerous because Thorin had been asking questions. She begged me to pick up her daughter, but when I arrived at the meet-up, it wasn't Ezra waiting for me—it was Thorin. He spat in my face, saying I would never have her. He must not know how my mind works.

Can't have her?

Well, challenge accepted.

I'd navigate in the shadows if I had to, and use every tool at my disposal, but I would have her if it were the last thing I did. Thorin would see that he had underestimated me.

Pretty early on, I learned that power was not given, but taken. My father, a man of influence and ruthlessness, had taught me the art of manipulation and control. Whatever lesson I failed to learn was embedded into my soul with a hot iron. Each scar, burned into the very fiber of my being.

By the time I had reached middle school, I had already orchestrated the downfall of several rivals, and I was always one step ahead. Maybe a part of me longed for something more, something real. Maybe that longing had found its focus in her, a beacon of light in this otherwise dark world. She was young and everything I wasn't—innocent, kind, and full of hope.

Facing down Thorin?

A man as formidable as my own father? That spit venom into the heart of the game, a game where strategy and sacrifice intertwine. I always enjoyed the thrill of it. Thorin's disdain and threats only fueled my resolve.

The council, however, was in his pocket, and trust was a luxury I didn't have. I was twenty-one then, just a kid, ostracized by Thorin and his cohorts. But I'm a very patient man, and time has worked in my favor.

One month after my thirty-first birthday, Ezra came to me and became my Luna.

That was a big mistake, little toy.

You are the most essential piece in this game. Breaking you was the promise, and you willingly gave yourself to me. The darkness within me whispered that destruction was inevitable.

After a decade of failed relationships, I realized I was destined to taint whatever I touched. So why, then, does your hatred inspire my own rage like liquid fire in my veins?

Perhaps, in the depths of our shared torment, there lies a twisted form of redemption. Your hatred, a mirror to my own self-loathing, ignited a fury that burns away the shadows within.

Could it be that we might find a semblance of salvation in our mutual destruction? Maybe our pain is a forge, and through this crucible, we might find a way to reshape the broken fragments of our souls. Whatever the cause, I couldn't deny that I was intrigued.

My fight has always been with Ezra's father, and Thorin switching sides allowed me to take what was mine. After all these years, I was no longer powerless. I was no longer weak.

But then, maybe neither was she? Her words echoed in my head. *"Don't go easy on me now."* What should have broken her somehow made her shine even brighter. It really was quite fascinating.

When her gaze met mine, it was brief, but it was enough to pull me back to reality. She flashed me a cocky smile and a middle finger before turning her attention back to her friends. *Oh, so you want to play, little toy—game on, then.*

"So happy you could join us, Luna. Although promptness doesn't seem to be of much importance to you, it seems. This is the second time now you've been late," I said, my voice loud enough to reach her where she stood.

She turned her attention back to me. "Did I inconvenience you?" she asked. "My apologies, Alpha."

While her words were sincere, her tone was anything but.

"Zayne? It's my understanding that you are quite a skilled warrior. While I know you are assigned to the personal protection of our Luna, can I trust you to oversee her training as well?" I asked as I approached.

"Yes, Alpha," he answered.

"Good. Gamma Dalton has volunteered to allow you to train with his platoon, but you alone are accountable for our Luna."

"Yes, Alpha." He bowed, and the three of them turned, heading towards Dalton. I don't think I'll ever get used to the formality of my new pack members. It's 2025, yet here this kid is, bowing to me. I know it's a sign of respect towards me as pack Alpha, but my pack of degenerates never showed that courtesy.

A few hours later, as I continued moving amongst the recruits, I watched as Ezra stepped up on the mat. She moved through the drills with anything but grace; her every motion was clumsy and weak. Her eyes kept darting to me, a mix of anger and something deeper flashing in the depths of those baby blue eyes.

Zayne, ever the observant protector, *how convenient*, noticed our exchange and began cracking jokes with her and the others.

"Alright, Ezra. Let's see if we can make this look like a dance. We need to find your rhythm; let the movements flow and turn this into something beautiful!" he called out to her, his voice carrying a hint of laughter as he began rolling his hips. But his humor wasn't going to keep her safe in this war, and her lack of training pissed me off.

"You're sloppy." My voice came out cold and measured, and I liked how it got a rise out of her. "If this were a real battle, you'd be dead."

I watched Ezra's jaw tighten, and then she turned all that burning anger on me, her eyes ablaze.

"Maybe if you spent less time criticizing and more time actually training us, we'd all be better off."

Yes. I grinned. *Ignite that flame, little one.*

The trainees all fell silent. The air was crackling with the intensity of our exchange. Zayne stepped between us, trying to defuse the situation, saying, "Hey now, let's save the fighting for our enemies, alright?"

My eyes flicked to Zayne briefly before locking back on Ezra. "Discipline is what keeps us alive," then turning to Zayne, "not jokes and jests."

Ezra took a step closer, pitting herself between me and Zayne, her voice low and fierce. "And hatred is what tears us apart. You'd do well to remember that, Alpha."

For a moment, the world seemed to hold its breath; the tension was discernable, and I was fighting the urge to grab hold of her…to feel those lips and her body pressed against mine.

The more she fought against me, the more I needed to show her who was in control. Having sex was never a part of the plan, but when she challenged me, it became inevitable.

My mind flashed again to last night—to the way it felt with her tight little pussy wrapped around my cock. To the sounds that seemed to tear from the chasm of her soul as I took what was mine—those sounds which had *haunted* my dreams and echoed through my mind even now. My mouth was watering, and I had to swallow back my desire to retake her.

Ezra's eyes were blazing with defiance as I stepped onto the mat. My demeanor remained calm despite the chaos brewing within me. The recruits formed a circle around us, wanting to watch their Alpha and Luna spar.

Now…this is a show. Let us teach them a lesson.

"I've been through hell and back. You don't scare me," Ezra spat, her voice dripping with venom.

My eyes darkened, a flicker of something intense passing through them. She should be. Still. "It's not about fear, little one. It's about understanding your limits and surpassing them. You're clumsy, ungraceful, and unbalanced."

"Oh, is that it?" she asked as she lunged forward with a right hook. I stopped it quickly, my hand wrapping around her fist and thrusting her hand back towards her.

"You're weak," I spat.

Ezra continued her advances on me. She fought with a ferocity born of anger, her movements wild and unpredictable. On the other hand, I was a master of precision; my every move was calculated to exploit her weaknesses.

The gathered recruits watched in awe as we sparred. With each punch and block, our bodies moved closer, the space between us shrinking until it was almost unbearable.

Finally, with a swift movement, I kicked her legs out from under her, catching her as she fell; I pinned her to the ground with my left arm while my right rested under her head. I leaned down, my breath hot against her ear as I spoke, "You fight with passion, my little toy, but you let your emotions control you. Until you learn to harness that fire, you'll never truly master it."

Ezra's chest heaved, her eyes locking onto mine, not shielding her fury. "I told you, I'm not your toy," she whispered, her voice trembling with the intensity of her emotions.

My grip tightened around the base of her neck, a movement she could feel, and no one else could see. She winced, and my breath was ragged when I spoke again.

"Let that hatred fuel you, but don't let it consume you."

For a moment, we stayed there, our bodies pressed together. When I finally pulled away, the recruits seemed to let out a collective breath they hadn't realized they were holding. Our harsh inhales and exhales filled the sudden silence and hung heavily in the air around us.

The lesson had been taught, the line drawn, but the fire between us had only begun to smolder. With a sharp exhale, I turned away. "Training is over for today. Everyone is dismissed."

"Hey!" she shouted, halting me in my tracks.

"I *can* do this," she said then, and a smile curved my lips as I walked out of the training grounds.

Ezra's POV

The recruits all began to disperse, murmuring amongst themselves. He had just made a fool of me in front of our entire pack. But he wasn't wrong. I was unskilled and easily overtaken by my emotions.

Goddess, why is he constantly fucking right? It's infuriating.

"Ezra?" Zayne helped me to my feet. "What did he say to you?"

"The same thing he's been telling me all week. That my emotions were going to get me killed, and I don't think he's wrong."

"Oh, fuck him, at least you have emotions," Kit said, locking her arm with mine.

"Yeah," was all I could say as I let her lead me out of the training grounds. I had emotions. Emotions that threatened to tear me apart every other second of the day. One second, I was okay. The next? I was sitting in a puddle of tears, questioning everything.

But when it came to Juno, I didn't know what to think. I'd never met a man so maddening. The way he carried himself was so cocky and indifferent at times; other times, he was cold, callous, and insensitive. But…

Heartless? Devoid of emotions?

I wasn't sure if I believed that. There was something hidden in those hazel eyes. A flicker of protectiveness that danced within. A possessive protectiveness—twisted and distorted, but undeniably present.

Maybe it was the need to feel something myself, anything other than the mind-numbing pain and sadness that had me so deep in thought. But I believed there was a line that even he wouldn't cross.

CHAPTER EIGHT

Maybe We Should Take Our Clothes Off And...

Ezra's POV

The following week didn't get any easier. I dislike the phrase *cat and mouse*, but it seemed to be the newest game we were playing, and I was clueless about the rules. I really wasn't sure who was the cat and who the mouse at this point. The more I tried to get to Juno, the further away he seemed to be, and the more frustrated I became.

He was keeping his distance, frustratingly unaffected by everything that had happened between us. He and Alec stayed locked up in the main office, except for training sessions. Which meant I still had no idea where Juno and I stood. A few times I thought about addressing *that* night, but then he'd flash a cocky smile in my direction, reminding me of just how much I shouldn't care.

So, in true Ezra fashion, I decided not to think about it, mostly. The truth is, if it were a one-off, it made it easier to ignore and bury in the past. I wasn't sure I could handle any more guilt after Bash, so it was better not to poke that particular beast. Instead, I did my best to keep my mind occupied, but that only seemed to get me so far these days.

The biggest problem with my strategy? The harder I pushed everything down, the louder it *screamed* for recognition, which often resulted in misplaced bursts of tears or anger that had Kit and Zayne afraid to leave my side now. I'm relatively sure a color-coded babysitting chart was involved. And while they collectively made an effective Band-Aid, it brought its own set of irritations with it.

For whatever reason, the more careful they were with my feelings, the more upset I became. I may be a walking time bomb, but the fact that everyone knew it? That made it so much worse somehow. You can't ignore the burden in your heart, put on a brave face, and lead the pack when the truth is written in every sympathetic expression on your friends' faces.

The air was getting thinner with each new day, and I felt like I was suffocating. I'd have to remind myself— breathe in, breathe out. It was the simplest of actions. It's the first thing you learn to do in your lifetime. Something so simple, even a baby can do it, and yet. If I didn't think about it, I couldn't do it.

It had been Kit's turn to watch me, when I officially lost my shit and burst through the pack house doors. She had mentioned something about how life had been different a few weeks ago, and how she missed it. I agreed with her. Life was eternally fucked now, because of my stupid mistakes, but it just had me thinking about the wrong decisions I had made.

I wish I could go back in time and rewrite history.

When I went quiet, she instantly regretted her words. She knew what that silence meant. She knew I was thinking about him and blaming myself for everything.

She began backtracking. Which, in reality, only made the entire situation worse. I couldn't listen to her words anymore. It didn't matter how she tried to fix it. Nothing would ever fix the fact that I was here, alone, without him. I couldn't think about it; I just needed to get as far away from it as possible.

Winter had officially fallen over Oakland, and the woods stood stark and skeletal against the pale sky as I fled through it, not ran—fled. The sunlight filtered through the bare branches in icy shards, cutting across my vision like cruel reminders of the world's frozen indifference to my unraveling.

The fractured beams were clawing at my back, threatening to expose the raw edges of my pain. My pulse quickened as the trail began to blur beneath my pounding feet. Each footstep crunched on the frozen ground, each sound a sharp, brittle echo that failed to drown the madness now clawing at my chest.

I wanted to be alone with my thoughts, but even here, the skeletal trees seemed to lean in, listening, judging. The wind howled through the branches, whispering truths I couldn't bear to face.

I pushed deeper, not towards anything, but away—away from the gnawing emptiness that threatened to consume me whole and the secrets I could never escape. Nothing felt real anymore. There was no real silence, no true escape—just the illusion of it, unraveling with every forced breath burning in my lungs.

Kit's voice, when it came, was a jarring intrusion. "Ezra, please! Slow down! You can't just keep running."

But she was wrong, I had to. I couldn't stop. Stopping would mean surrendering to the darkness, letting it swallow me whole, and I wasn't ready to face it. I loved her, but her presence was a mirror. It was all I could see when I looked at her, that hollowness reflecting back at me as I desperately tried to ignore it.

"I'm fine, Kit, just go back," I screamed into the night.

We both knew those words were a lie. I was anything but fine these days. Even as I said it, Junior's words played through my mind.

"Cry for him, mourn his loss, this once. Then, pick yourself up and forget it. This weakness will kill us all."

This weakness. *My* weakness. I knew he was right…*again*. I couldn't afford to let my emotions take over, and yet I had never felt so fragile.

The woods became a blur of grey and white as I pushed harder; each stride fueled by the need to outrun the shadows nipping at my heels. Kit's panicked pleas soon faded, swallowed up by the biting wind and lost to the distance between us.

I could almost taste the freedom, feel it brushing against my skin like a phantom chill, but the woods, ever watchful, had other plans.

A gnarled and unforgiving root snaked across the path, hidden beneath the snow. My foot caught under it, and the world tilted violently, sending me crashing into the frozen earth. All at once, the air rushed from my lungs, leaving me gasping and broken. And then, the dam burst.

Tears cascaded down my cheeks, cold and relentless, mingling with the ice and snow. Every darkened thought, every fear, and every unspoken word erupted from the depths of my soul in a torrent of pain as the light surrendered to the horizon, and the night fell around me.

I felt like a shattered mosaic scattered across the frozen forest floor, with no hope of ever piecing myself back together.

As I lay there, cradled by the unforgiving cold, a siren song of release echoed in my heart. The cold whispered promises of oblivion, and I wondered.

Would it be so bad to surrender to its icy embrace?

As my eyelids fluttered, heavy with the weight of every frozen tear shed, I began to yearn for it. I craved the cessation of pain that would bring the end of all this guilt, of all this loneliness, of all this hurt.

"Ezra, get up."

"No. Lana, I can't do this anymore."

"This is not our time."

Visions flickered behind my eyes: shared secrets under starry skies on the bridge overlooking the river, the fragrant flowers of the greenhouse, and the warmth of his hand in mine. Memories that were once a source of such joy pierced through me like broken shards now.

"Where are you?" I screamed into the night. "You swore you would hold me again, but you can't, cause you're gone!! You *left* me, and I can't do this without you."

Each memory was a cruel reminder of what I had lost and would never have again. Unmoving, I existed beyond the tick of clocks, adrift in timelessness. I no longer had feeling in my fingertips. My face, which had felt so cold, was numb now when a whisper of him carried on the wind, urging me to get up, to continue to fight, to live.

The cold intensified, but now, it felt different. It didn't feel like a peaceful surrender, but a challenge. Adrenaline coursed through my veins, as a primal instinct to survive, to protect the flame of hope, flickered to life within.

Metaphorically, of course.

I was chilled to the bone, and I would have killed for the warmth of a fire. I willed myself to move, cursing under my breath as I pushed myself up from the frozen earth. My body screamed in protest, the ground biting into my palms like needles.

A branch snapping to my left echoed through the silence as I gathered my footing.

My heart pounded against my ribs, my pulse drumming in my ears as I squinted into the darkness. Every shadow seemed to writhe, every rustle of leaves sounded like approaching footsteps. I held my breath, straining to hear, to see, to discern the intention behind the sound.

Then, a pair of eyes gleamed in the darkness, and a low growl rumbled through the trees, promising a confrontation as inevitable as the coming dawn. I stumbled back, reemerging into the moon's veiled glow, its light fracturing through the trees.

"Are you going to just stand there in the shadows? Show yourself!"

He started chuckling as he stepped forward. "We really need to stop meeting like this, princess."

"Juno? You scared the shit out of me, what are you even doing out here?"

"Looking for you, Kit was afraid you'd…"

"What? Kill myself? Hardly, I was enjoying the quiet."

"Sure. Well, are you done? Here, take my coat." He pushed it toward me.

"I'm good," I said, eyeing him up and down. As much as I'd kill for the warmth, I didn't want a damn thing from that man.

"Suit yourself, but it's late. Let's go, princess."

He pulled his cellphone out of his pocket, quickly typing a message before shoving it back into his pants. When I stood there simply glaring at him, he rolled his eyes.

"What?"

"I told you I'm no princess."

"No kidding. Brat might be more accurate."

"I am not a brat!"

"I don't know, making your friends worry about you enough to drag me out of bed—obnoxiously, I might add— makes you a brat."

"I am not a brat, and they have no reason to worry. I'm *fine*. And I can get myself home."

I began looking around. Realistically, everything had been a blur up to this point, and... I wasn't sure which way I had come from. The fresh-fallen snow shimmered in the pale moonlight, covering any remnants of the tracks I had made. I was, in fact, lost. Not that I was willing to admit that fact to him.

"This way," he muttered, seizing my hand, his touch a fleeting spark against my frozen skin. A disgruntled sigh escaped his lips as he released me. "Put it on."

Before I could protest, his coat was draped over my shivering shoulders, his hands moving with brisk urgency, rubbing up and down my arms.

"Friction will help warm you," he explained. "How long were you lying on the ground like that?"

"I... you saw that? I honestly don't know," I confessed, my voice a mere whisper.

"Maybe we should take off our clothes and…" he began, a glint of something unreadable in his eyes.

"Uh...No, absolutely not."

"You're teetering on the edge of hypothermia," he countered, "it would help you warm up quicker."

"No," I insisted, my resolve hardening against his unsettling proposition.

"Fine, have it your way," he conceded, though a hint of amusement lingered in his tone.

In a swift motion, he scooped me into his arms and began to run, his strides powerful and unwavering. When we arrived at the pack house, he carried me straight into the library on the left, swaddling me in a blanket as soft and warm as a lover's embrace.

I watched as he piled kindling into the fireplace, coaxing the flames to life with practiced ease.

"Let me get this going," he said, his voice softening, "and then we'll have a nurse examine you."

"Why are you doing this?" I asked, my voice laced with suspicion.

"Well, you made it pretty clear you weren't willing to part with your clothes, so…Fire," he said, pushing his hands toward the flames sarcastically.

If he wasn't such an ass, it might have been endearing.

"Don't worry," he replied, a smirk playing on his lips, "there's plenty of time for you to hate me tomorrow."

"Why?" I pressed.

"Why, what?" he countered, his eyes dancing with a hint of mischief.

"Why do you want me to hate you?" I clarified, my gaze unwavering, seeking to unravel the mystery of his intentions. The silence droned on, and he said nothing as he finished loading logs into the fireplace.

"Stay here," he warned, ignoring my question. The doors flung open as he stood up. Kit came running in, hugging me tightly to her chest, followed by Zayne.

"You are in so much trouble, young lady," Kit said, pulling back to push her finger into my chest.

"Ow," I said, rubbing the spot where her finger dug in.

The clinking of the doors as they shut had me looking past her to where Juno had just stood, but just like that, he was gone.

CHAPTER NINE

What Did I Tell You, Little One?

Ezra's POV

"There's my girl!" Kit shrieked, her footsteps echoing as she sprinted toward Zayne and me. She was moving so quickly, she bumped shoulders with a girl I'd never seen before.

"Watch it," the girl spat, disgust twisting her lips as her gaze raked over my best friend.

"Hey, my bad, I didn't see—" Kit began, but the girl cut her off. Her words were loud, piercing through the hum of the wolves in the hallway.

"You know that's the problem with all of you Night Tree wolves, you don't see anything or anyone except yourself."

"I really didn't mean to—" Kit started again.

"And I really don't care."

"Excuse me?" Kit challenged. "And who the fuck are you?"

The girl smirked. "Someone you don't need to worry about." She paused, her gaze flicking toward me. "Yet."

With that cryptic as fuck response, she turned, melting into the group of people leaving the training grounds.

I wasn't allowed to attend the last few days. I was basically on house arrest after my little outing. The nurse felt I needed a couple of days to let my body recover before resuming training, and Juno banned me from the grounds to ensure that it happened.

Kit still went, but Zayne refused to leave my side, so he got to play hooky with me. We mostly hung out in the library or went for walks while the others trained. Then, we always met up with Kit afterward.

"What was that about?" Zayne asked, his voice laced with concern as we reached Kit.

"I don't know," she admitted, looking both pissed off and confused by the entire situation. "Anyway, how are you feeling? Everything go okay today?"

"Oh yes, behaving and everything," I teased.

Zayne laughed before adding, "I don't know, I kind of miss training, the pack house is so quiet during the day. It's weird."

"Don't worry, house arrest should end tomorrow," I said, bumping his shoulder.

Kit sighed heavily. "Oh, thank the Goddess, I really miss you guys!"

"I miss you, too, Kit, but I need to go see Junior. Can I meet up with you guys later?" I asked quickly as I turned to run away, not really wanting an answer to that question. Zayne's hand on my arm stopped me abruptly. His face was telling me everything he needed me to hear without even saying a word.

"I'm okay, really; I know you want to keep an eye on me," I said, placing my hand over his, which still firmly gripped my arm. His grip wasn't painful, but more protective. "I love you for that, Zayne, but I need to speak with our Alpha alone. You can't protect me from that."

Zayne stepped forward, placing his hands on my shoulders. "Every time you're alone with that prick, something bad happens," he spat.

"Zayne, I'm not asking."

"Fine, but I'm coming with you."

"I'm really okay, the nurse cleared me, and I promise to go straight there, then straight back to my room." I paused before adding. "Besides, Kit needs your help."

"I uh…do?" she asked.

"Yeah, you know, with that thing you told me about?" I shot Kit a pointed look over Zayne's shoulder, hoping she'd catch on.

"Oh, right! That thing," Kit replied, catching my drift. I could tell she wasn't sure about helping me, but bestie status prevailed. "I almost forgot, but yeah, I could really use your expertise, Zayne."

I mouthed *thank you* at her as I wiggled out of Zayne's grip. Kit was usually pretty good at making things up on the fly, and there was definitely something going on there.

Why couldn't I play cupid *and* address my current entanglements? I mean, I'm killing two birds with one stone here.

Zayne hesitated, glancing between us. Then he sighed, defeated. "Alright, fine. Lead the way," he said to Kit, who happily pulled him away.

I couldn't help but smile after them; I liked the idea of them as a couple. Kit has always been a momma figure to me. Somehow, Zayne had become my safe place. They fit, like the mom and dad I never had.

I made my way to Juno's office, but it was empty, so I decided to check his room. When I got there, I hesitated before lifting my fist, suddenly nervous. I was dreading the conversation we were about to have, but I needed to put on my big-girl panties and have an actual, honest conversation with him.

I tapped the door lightly, but there was no response. I knocked again, louder this time. Mid-knock, it opened.

Juno stepped out into the hall, closing the door behind him. He folded his arms across his chest and said nothing as he stared down at me.

"Can I come in?" I asked.

"No."

"Well, why the hell not? I need to talk to you!"

That might be a new record, not even thirty seconds in, and he already triggered me with one word. I mean, really? *Fuck this guy!*

He just grinned at me. "Is there another reason you'd like to come into my room, little one?" he asked, looking amused—*cocky little shit.*

"Juno, I'm serious. I need to talk to you," I said, calmer this time.

His grin faded slightly, but his eyes still held that infuriating glint. "And what exactly do you want to sort out?"

"Everything," I said, my voice trembling. "We can't keep doing this. The mind games are tearing me apart."

"I'm not playing mind games."

"Oh, really? So, what was last night?"

For a moment, he just stared at me, his expression unreadable. Then, with a sigh, he unfolded his arms and stepped aside. "Fine. Come in. Let's talk."

I stepped into his room, and the look of it surprised me. I don't know what I was expecting. Just darker.

Emptier? More simplistic? He was so secretive, but the walls had been freshly painted, a deep blue. It was calming, like the twilight sky just before nightfall. Shelves lined the far wall, filled with books of various genres, their spines worn and well-loved. A large wooden desk sat against another wall, cluttered with papers, notebooks, and binders in perfect symmetrical stacks.

His bed was neatly made, covered with a dark grey comforter and several mismatched pillows. A soft, woven rug lay on the floor, adding a touch of warmth to the room. In one corner, sat a bunch of painted canvases, the vibrant hues heightened by the soft light of a nearby lamp. The room smelled of cedar and something else uniquely Juno.

The space was personal and unexpectedly inviting. A stark contrast to his personality.

I turned, and when I went to speak, he was so close that my breath hitched in my throat. His familiar silence began to bring a strange sense of comfort.

He had come to my room the last two nights to check on me.

The first night, he said nothing. He tucked me into bed, a ghost of a presence, and then vanished.

Last night mirrored the first, a silent ritual of tucking me in. But as he turned to leave, his hand lingered, gently sweeping stray hairs behind my ear. His touch, a featherlight caress, hovered there, his thumb tracing the curve of my cheek.

His eyes, usually a kaleidoscope of green and brown, were now depths of shadowed obsidian.

His fingers drifted to the mark on my neck—the jagged brand he had carved with his knife. A tremor ran through him, and I could have sworn I heard a strangled groan escape his lips.

His touch was a spark against tinder, igniting something within me, which left me unsure of how to react. Why was there both a sense of longing and revulsion? I was a walking contradiction, my body betraying my mind.

How could I simultaneously hate and crave this man? How could he inflict such pain on one occasion and then offer such unexpected tenderness in others?

"First thing's first," he finally rasped, his voice a low, gravelly rumble that sent shivers down my spine.

His hand shot out, gripping the back of my neck with possessive force. He crashed his lips against mine, a brutal claiming that stole my breath. I pulled back, desperate to break free, but his other hand shot out, his fingers pinching my face, holding me captive. A primal growl, raw and possessive, tore from his throat, and a knot of fear and reluctant desire twisted in the pit of my stomach.

"Juno?" I asked, breathless.

"What did I tell you, little one?" His voice was so deep, so demanding. *What did he tell me?* He hasn't said a word to me in so long, my mind was racing.

I didn't get a chance to respond. He leaned down, parting my lips with his tongue. The slick wetness of it, mixed with his breath, was cold and sent a shiver down my spine.

Lana snorted, clearly annoyed by my lack of self-control, and I was glad, because it pulled me back to reality.

No. This can't happen again. I came here to talk, not make out.

I pushed him hard away from me, and he laughed as he gathered his footing. Licking his lips and moving his thumb over them, that signature cocky smile spreading to his eyes as he leaned back against the desk.

"Seriously, Juno?"

"It's not my fault that you look so deceptively sweet." He laughed.

"It's not a deception; I'm as sweet as fucking cotton candy!" I said firmly.

"Cotton candy? Well, I'm craving something sweet. Come melt in my mouth, little one," he said.

My jaw fell open as I stared at him in disbelief.

Before I could say another word, my phone rang. When I saw the name on the screen, I turned it to show Juno. It was Gabe.

"Answer it, but don't let him push you," he said. I rolled my eyes and answered the phone, putting it on speaker.

"Gabriel?"

"Hello, kitten, so good to hear your voice."

Lana was growling. *"Oh, you hate Gabe, but with Juno. You are quiet as shit?"* I taunted.

"Juno's not a threat. Gabe is," she replied, annoyance in her tone.

She had gone radio silent since my little late-night stroll. She wasn't happy with me, and to be honest, the fact that I had let myself fall apart like that? Left a lot of room for self-loathing.

Turning back to the conversation with Gabe, I finally spoke.

"How are you feeling?" I taunted. "How's your stomach?"

"A beautiful reminder of what's to come, kitten. But make no mistake, you will pay for that one."

"What do you want?" I asked, annoyance now lingering in my tone.

"I found something, well, a few somethings. Or rather, *someone's*, I think, might belong to you."

111

My eyes darted to Juno, and he mouthed *scouts* at me. His expression mirrored my horror. We never heard back from the scouts. I was so wrapped up in my *feelings* that I had forgotten that he sent them the night before. Nor did I notice they never returned.

Every passing day, I wonder more and more if I'm the right person for this.

"Don't worry," he continued when I stopped speaking. "They are fine. For now."

"But?" I asked.

"But you will meet me, or you'll be the reason they take their last breath." I looked up at Juno, and he mouthed *FUCK NO* at me.

"And they'll be unharmed?" I questioned, ignoring Juno's warning. Angrily, he grabbed the phone out of my hand.

"That's not happening. You have matters to discuss; you talk to me," he growled into the phone, his voice a menacing rumble that promised no mercy. There was no response, just a *distinct* click as the line disconnected.

"What the fuck, Juno! He is gonna kill them!" I shouted.

"There is no way in hell you're meeting with him, and that's final. Do you ever use that beautiful fucking head of yours? Or is it just for show?" His voice was so calm. Unbothered by the fact that he had just sentenced the scouts to their deaths by intervening in that call. But quick to point out another of my damn flaws.

"That wasn't your choice to make."

"They knew what they were signing up for. If they die, let's hope they do it in silence."

"Do you hear yourself right now?!" I was beyond livid.

I went to snatch my phone back, and he lifted it above his head and gave me a stern look. "You will not call him back."

"Give me my damn phone, Juno."

He lowered it slowly, but before he returned it, he said, "I mean it, little one. You will not call him back, or I'll make you regret going against my order. Loyalty. You promised me that much."

"Fuck you, their death is on you then. Not me," I said, grabbing my phone from his hand and turning to leave.

One step.

I went one fucking step before he grabbed me, his hands on my hips, spinning me around, his hand lifting my chin to meet his eyes.

"I will always protect what is mine," he said, his voice a solemn vow. "Promise me you won't call him."

"Fine. I fucking promise. Can I go now?"

His eyes never left mine. "This isn't on you, dolly."

He released me after what felt like an eternity. I stumbled back, my heart pounding like a war drum in my chest. If the anger behind my eyes was literal, he'd have been burnt to a fucking crisp. This wasn't the first time he'd said that. He had already told me that he would protect what was his before.

He often left my mind foggy, with so many unanswered questions buzzing around, but today, one constant became clear: I was his. We both knew it, and I hated him for it. The air felt heavier now as I walked away, knowing that his words would linger with me forever.

To him, my life was more valuable than the scouts. He killed them to save me.

"*As he should.*" Lana's voice rang out.

"*Seriously? Whose fucking side are you on?*" I asked as I made my way down the hallway to my room.

"*I'm always on your side, but he isn't wrong. As Luna, your life will always be placed above others.*"

"*I should've died with him.*"

"*It was not our time.*"

"*The Moon Goddess tell you that?*"

"*No, Kane…*"

I felt a pang in my chest, reminding me that I wasn't the only one who lost their mate. Lana had lost her mate, too. My pace slowed as I soothed my wolf.

"*We will avenge them.*"

"Of course we will. We're survivors."

CHAPTER TEN

Get The Alpha, Tell Him We've Caught a Kitten.

Ezra's POV

"Ezra," Lana growled in warning.

"What? He made me promise not to call him back. So, I won't, but I will not just sit here while they die."

"This is the worst idea you've ever had, which is saying something."

"Thanks for the unwavering support."

"This is foolishness."

"Shut up."

"And rude, too."

Rolling my eyes, I climbed through the window and lowered myself off the ledge. Been here, done this before. Never thought I'd be dumb enough to fall from a second-story window again, at least, not on purpose. However, repeating mistakes was a normal behavior for me lately.

At least I wasn't falling on concrete this time. I let go, falling to the ground.

"Fuck, I had to be part dog?"

Lana's growling made me chuckle. *"What? Cats land on their feet, don't they?"*

"Even a cat couldn't help your lack of coordination."

I dipped my head low as I walked through the underbrush to the garage. When I saw Bash's bike, I couldn't help but smile. It hadn't moved for weeks, but in the moon's glow, it seemed to shimmer with a life of its own. Whispering tales of adventures past and journeys yet to come. All the memories were still fresh wounds, but ones that held so much joy, and this black beauty had grown on me over the past year.

I'll admit it was much heavier than I initially thought it would be. Bash always made it look so easy. As I struggled against the bike's weight, I considered taking my car, but I didn't want the engine to give me away, alerting Junior to my late-night activities. The bike, while heavy, was still the safest bet.

But holy shit. *This was a bad idea.*

"Why do you refuse to shift? We could travel much faster on foot."

"I can do this on my own."

"I need to stretch my feet, let me out."

"I'm not ready."

The garage was far enough from the main pack house that I doubt anyone would hear the bike start up, but still, I pushed it on foot to the main gate. Jumping on, I let it coast down the hill until I was a safer distance from the pack house, about a mile down the road. I turned the key, pulled in the clutch, and hit the ignition switch, letting it roar to life.

The familiar hum hit my ears, and it was like the world opened up before me. The vibrations resonated through my bones, a reminder of the freedom I'd felt with Bash on the open road. He had taught me how to ride, but this was my first solo mission, and to say I was nervous was an understatement.

The hum was a comforting reminder of him. Weirdly, it made me feel like he was here with me, even with the air growing thick with tension, and every shadow catching my eye as a potential threat. I felt at peace as I inched closer to the Silver Pack territory.

Once the glow of the pack house came into view, I stopped, hiding the bike on an access road, and decided to make the rest of the journey on foot. As I neared the border, a branch snapped underfoot, and I froze, my breath catching in my throat. Another few steps, and I was surrounded, the gleaming eyes of wolves reflecting the moonlight like shards of ice.

The wolf in charge, a towering figure with a scarred muzzle, stepped forward. His growl was a low rumble that sent shivers down my spine.

"Ezra," he snarled; his teeth bared in a menacing grin.

"Oh shit, is that you, Tommy boy?" I asked, sarcastically. My eyes scanned the wolves around me, searching for a way to escape if needed, but it was too late. The wolves were keeping a tight formation, and I was vastly outnumbered.

"Gabe will be pleased to have his little kitten back." He laughed.

"Be careful," I said, releasing my claws. "Kittens tend to scratch, but then it looks like you've already learned that lesson."

"You're alone? I'd say you're either incredibly brave or foolish." He smirked, a glint of challenge in his eyes. "So, which one is it?"

"I want my scouts released," I said, planting my feet in the gravel for better traction, in case this goes south.

He narrowed his eyes, considering my demand. "And why should I comply? What's in it for me?"

"I'm afraid that this demand is above your pay grade. I want to see Gabe."

He hesitated, the authority in his stance wavering. "Fine," he muttered, "but don't make me regret this. Micky? Get the Alpha, tell him we've caught a kitten." He smiled.

The wolf to his left, Micky, I presume, took off, heading to the gate down the road. Thomas shifted back to his human form and held his hand to me. "Shall we?"

I strained my neck, looking up at the massive man in front of me. I had almost forgotten how absurdly large this man was; his presence was intimidating. Still, I wasn't leaving here without my scouts.

"We should do Gabriel a favor and rid him of this headache," a she-wolf on the right growled, stepping forward.

"Alpha wants her unharmed. So, you will remember your place and stand down, Kate," he snapped in her direction. She instinctively lowered her head, a sign of respect to her Beta, although she kept her teeth bared.

"I'll go with you peacefully, Tommy Boy. There's no need to hold hands." I laughed as I stepped forward. I wouldn't let him or this little she-wolf intimidate me.

I turned to her. "Such a good girl."

My comment annoyed her further, causing her to snarl. I shouldn't be making more enemies on purpose, but since she already has it in for me, I didn't see any harm in it.

"Fine," Thomas said, turning halfway, ushering me ahead. He placed a black, satin sack over my head when I stepped forward. *Well shit.*

"Is this fucking necessary?" I asked as my hands were yanked behind my back and secured in metal cuffs.

"You're the enemy, so I'd say precautions should be expected." He laughed as he snugged the cuffs down. "Besides, I've heard stories, and I know how you like to be treated, how much of a *good girl* you can be when properly motivated. If you weren't my Alpha's property, I'd offer you ten reasons to be a good girl and take my cock right now."

"You really are dense, aren't you? I'm not Gabe's property," I hissed back. "And ten reasons?"

"I know you were an obedient kitten once. Gabe never expected this resistance; he thought he had gotten rid of those pesky friends of yours, but they keep popping up, causing problems, and getting in the way. Yet, it has to be you. He says you'll be worth the headache, but I'm having doubts. Yes, ten, sweetheart. If you're a good girl, I'll let you choke on them."

"Gross, I wouldn't let you near me with a ten-foot pole." I laughed. Considering how the world spun in a dizzying blur when his backhand connected with a sickening thud, I'd say he didn't find that as funny as I did.

It was forceful enough that my vision shattered into fragments of light and shadow, of pain and confusion. The force sent me reeling, my body flung like a ragdoll to the unforgiving gravel road below. The rough stones were biting into my skin. I'm sure there would be some wonderful brush burns left there. The taste of blood lingered on my lips, mingling with the dust and grit, now enveloping the inside of the sack covering my head.

Slowly, the world began to stabilize, and the ringing in my ears faded to a dull roar. Pain radiated from the point of impact, but I wasn't focused on that.

"You're all dead," the achingly familiar voice rang out. As I lay there, the gravel pressing into my back, I could make out the sounds of tearing flesh. The piercing screams that were quickly silenced as the scent of blood flooded my nostrils. Determined, I sat up, despite the agony. Still blind to the scene unfolding around me.

It couldn't be him, could it? He couldn't possibly know that I was here. I was so careful. I didn't tell anyone where I was going. But it sounded like him, familiar, like a distant anchor in chaos.

"You're outnumbered," Thomas' voice called out.

"Makes no difference to me, you're still going to die."

The screams of the wolves, their cries of agony as they were torn apart, chilled me to my core. Each howl sliced through the chaos around me until it ended abruptly. Thumps and thuds sounded out, no doubt the multitude of bodies and various body parts hitting the gravel road. As those awful noises enveloped me, the adrenaline coursing through my veins almost heightened my senses, making every moment more vivid, more alive, but distorted by the black canvas, it felt like I was trapped in a dream again.

The scent of blood mixed with sweat invaded my nostrils, and I was feeling sick. That was until I felt arms wrapping around me, pulling me backwards, shocking my system, and pulling me back to reality.

"JUNO," I screamed, as I struggled against the person pulling me back, doubling down on the fact that it was him out there.

A fierce cry rang out, and the arms around me lost their grasp. After a bustle of movement, everything went quiet apart from the single set of footfalls heading toward me on the gravel. The black bag was ripped off my head.

"Juno…" I said, breathlessly, as my eyes adjusted to the light. The blood pulsing through my veins was unrelenting, matching the wild energy in his eyes. Crimson stained his hands and the tattered remnants of his clothes, which clung to his body like a second skin.

It wasn't the massacre of wolves around me that gained my focus. I was locked in on his eyes, and the burning rage simmering within them. The lines of his face were taut, his jaw clenched, his breath ragged as he stared down at me. But there was something more, below the surface.

His hand grazed my lip, and he cursed under his breath, abruptly turning his back on me. He kicked at the gravel with a forceful frustration, his hands clenched tightly at his sides, resembling a young boy in the throes of a temper tantrum. The raw, childlike innocence was something I had never witnessed before.

He was a canvas of claw marks soaked in blood. Yet, the mere sight of a single drop of blood on my lip seemed to unravel him completely, as if it threatened to tear his very soul apart.

"Juno, I..."

"What the FUCK IS WRONG WITH YOU?"

I didn't know what to say as he stormed back to me, staring down at me like a father scolding his young child. He just tore through half a dozen wolves…Thomas included. Gabe's Beta. That wouldn't go unanswered. Did he not understand what he had just done? This was bad, this was so unbelievably bad. Yet, he was scolding *me*?

Usually, I'd be quick to anger, but something about the look in his eyes softened the storm within me, a whisper of vulnerability that I couldn't ignore. Getting to my feet, I looked up at him, my hands still secured behind my back.

"What's wrong with me? Have you given any thought to what you've just done?" I asked, my voice calm and steady. Hey, maybe I'm making progress? Getting control over my emotions has been a struggle lately, especially with Junior.

He looked me up and down, like I had lost my mind. "You mean save your life?"

And just like that, the anger flared up again. Is he serious right now? He wasn't even supposed to be here. "Excuse me? I was fine, but you just killed Gabe's Beta."

He scoffed. "Fine?! You were FINE?! Look at what he did to you…"

I glanced down at the bruises and cuts marring my skin from the gravel, the evidence of the struggle still fresh. "I had it under control," I insisted, though a tremor in my voice betrayed me.

"Under control? You call that under control?" He took a step closer, his eyes blazing. "I couldn't stand by and watch you get hurt."

"You don't get to decide that!" I shouted back, my frustration bubbling over. "I didn't ask for your help, and this is nothing; it's not like he was going to kill me. He was taking me to Gabe."

"AND YOU THINK THAT'S ANY BETTER? Dammit, dolly. You are such an absolute pain in my ass, you know that?!"

"I could say the same for you!!! What do you think is going to happen to the scouts now?"

"For fuck's sake, you came here to try to save them? They are already dead. Guaranteed. And you would've walked right in, giving him the one thing he could use to destroy our pack!"

"Juno," I began, but he was clearly done talking. He picked me up and started walking back into the woods. "Juno, he isn't going to forgive this."

He shook his head, the disbelief etched on his face. "You think I give a damn about Gabe's forgiveness?"

The silence that followed was almost deafening. Leaves crunched underfoot, branches snapped as he cleared a path forward, and each heartbeat echoed the unyielding tension between us.

"Juno, Bash's bike, we have to go back. I have to get the bike."

"It's gone. Forget it."

"JUNO!" I yelled forcefully, and he let out a frustrated grunt. He set me down, pushed a palm to his forehead, and rubbed his temples. "Where is it?"

"Wait, what?"

"Where is the damn bike, Ezra?"

"About a mile from the Silver Pack grounds, hidden on an old access road."

"I'll come back for it, but first, you're going home, where I can keep you safe."

As he made his way through the woods, cradling me in his arms like a fragile child, I looked up at this man, the man I couldn't help but fight with. This man, I couldn't quite figure out.

"Thank you," I whispered.

No response. We continued in silence until the woods gave way to the road. Alec and Zayne were perched against the side of a black SUV.

"I told you to call if you needed backup," Alec said as we approached, looking us up and down.

"I didn't need it," Juno responded. "But can you take the cuffs off?"

"Sure thing, Alpha," he said, pulling out his keychain and using the small cuff key to remove the cuffs.

"Do you always just walk around with cuff keys on your person?" I asked, rubbing my sore wrists.

"They come in handy, occasionally." Alec laughed, tossing the keys and catching them before shimmying them back into his pocket.

After being released from the cuffs, I smiled at Alec and approached Zayne cautiously. I knew this wouldn't be a pleasant conversation. I had left my Gamma and snuck out, and I still didn't know how these men had found me. His back was turned to me, his shoulders tense and rigid, a clear sign of his simmering anger, rightfully so. I took a deep breath. I was struggling to find the words, but I knew I needed to fix this.

"Zayne," I began softly, but he spun around, eyes blazing.

"Why, Ezra? Why do you always do this?" His voice was more hurt than angry, but each word cut deep. "You put yourself in danger again, and didn't trust me enough to tell me. Do you have any idea how that makes me feel?"

I flinched at his words. Guilt. An overabundance of guilt hit me head-on. "I didn't want to drag you into it. I thought I could handle it on my own."

"That's the problem, Ez."

He took a step closer, his expression a storm of emotions now. "We're supposed to be friends, and friends trust each other. They don't keep secrets and run headfirst into danger alone."

"I didn't mean to—" I started, but he cut me off again. Not done grilling me yet.

"Didn't mean to what? Make me worry sick about you? Make me feel like our friendship means nothing to you?" his voice softened slightly; the hurt more evident now. "I thought we were a team. You and I, together. But every time you do this, it feels like you're pushing me away. I want to protect you. I want to help you. I'm always here for you, haven't I proved that yet?"

I could feel the tears filling my eyes now, threatening to break free. He was right, he was always there for me, and I knew why he was Bash's best friend. Zayne was fiercely loyal, dependable, and incredibly strong.

Honestly, I wouldn't have made it this far without him. It didn't matter how broken I felt without Bash. Zayne was always there to pick up the pieces.

Hurting him was never my intention, but besides Kit? I wasn't used to having people who cared about me. "Zayne, I didn't realize how much I was hurting you. I just…I didn't want you to get hurt because of me, too. I'm so sorry."

He sighed, and it seemed like the anger was slowly ebbing away, replaced by a deep sadness. "Ezra, I'd rather face danger with you than be left in the dark, wondering if you're okay. But you have to trust me enough to let me in. Bash's death…it wasn't your fault."

I nodded, the tears were streaming down my face, when he pulled me into a hug, holding me tightly—the way only Zayne could. "Shhh…it's okay. Please don't cry. Just don't shut me out again, okay? We're in this together."

In Zayne's embrace, amidst the lingering tension and unspoken fears, a fragile understanding began to mend the rift between us.

But it was short-lived.

"Come on, we need to get her home," Juno said, opening the door for me and patting Zayne's shoulder. I slid in, and he shut it behind me, but I could have sworn I heard Zayne thanking Juno before they made their way around the car. Great, they finally had some common ground—hating my life choices.

CHAPTER ELEVEN

Well, Shit. I Liked This Shirt.

Ezra's POV

The ride back to the pack house was nauseating, to say the least, and eerily silent. Leaving my mind to wander. I hated everything about tonight. I tried to save our scouts, but all I managed to do was hurt both Zayne and Juno.

Tonight's events were weighing heavily on my mind. Every little bump in the road seemed to echo the turmoil in my heart. The silence was suffocating, as I kept replaying the events in my mind, wishing I could turn back time.

Zayne's pained expression and Juno's bloodied form haunted me. I had set out hoping to save our scouts in time, but instead, it felt like I had led us all into a nightmare—another failure as Luna for Storm Cross pack. How many strikes do you get before they vote you off the island?

"You know you shouldn't have gone alone. You know that, right?" Juno asked, breaking through the silence.

"I didn't think it would end like this…"

"That's the problem, you didn't think!" Junior's voice rose. "Do you have any idea what could have happened?"

I take back what I said. Please bring back the silence.

"I tried to warn you," Lana piped in.

"Not you too. Shush."

The argument only escalated from there, words flying like daggers. Soon, accusations and regrets were all that filled the small space in the car, each one cutting deeper than the last. My defenses crumbled under Junior's fury, but I stood my ground, trying to explain my actions. His retorts quickly met all of mine, further proving his point.

The pack house came into view, and I quickly jumped out of the car, stomping up the long stairs to the main entrance. Yes, I understand that was an incredibly childish thing to do. Did I care? Not in the slightest.

I couldn't stand that smug attitude of his or the way he's always so egotistical, thinking he's better than everyone else. It's like he has this permanent smirk on his perfect fucking face that screams with arrogance.

It sure as fuck doesn't help that he is usually always right. It's true, I wasn't thinking about anything besides saving the scouts, but did he need to be that relentless and unforgiving about the situation? Did it matter that my heart was in the right place, even if the execution sucked?

No, it didn't matter; whatever damage became of this was on me. Gabe was already pissed, and the death of his Beta was going to push him over the edge.

Juno may have dealt the lethal blow, but his being there was all *my* fault.

The image of him standing over me would be forever burned into my mind after tonight, too. What's even more infuriating? How the sight of him had me craving him in ways I hated.

There was something about those broad shoulders and the way his bloodied shirt clung to them that had me soaking through my panties. Add that cocky smile, and I stood no chance at slowing my racing heart. It was maddening how I couldn't help but be drawn to him.

Juno's POV

I quickly got out when she slammed the door. I was about to go after her when Zayne grabbed my bicep, pulling me to a halt.

"Maybe just give her some space, let me talk to her..."

I looked down at his hand, and he quickly pulled it away.

"You…care about her, don't you?" Zayne's eyes glinted with a knowing smirk.

"She's my Luna."

"Yeah, sure. I bet that's why you're acting like a jealous boyfriend right now," Zayne poked, his tone dripping with sarcasm, and it took everything I had not to level the little fuck. "Maybe you could try going a little easier on her. She's been through a lot, you know."

"She doesn't need me to baby her. You do that enough for both of us," I snapped, my jaw tightening as I walked around to the car's trunk. "Besides, you don't know what you're talking about."

I removed the bloodied, ripped shirt I was wearing and replaced it with a clean t-shirt from the trunk.

"Oh, don't I?" Zayne leaned in, his smirk widening. "It's written all over your face, man. Every time she walks into a room, you can't help but watch her. And the way you bristle when someone else gets too close…it's pretty obvious."

"He's got a point," Alec chimed in, folding his arms over his chest.

"Back off, both of you."

Zayne chuckled, holding up his hands in mock surrender. "Hey, relax. I'm just saying, maybe you should tell her. Might make things a bit easier, you know?"

I took a deep breath, my eyes narrowing as I tried to steady my emotions. "She's so damn stubborn, how doesn't she fucking get it?"

"Oh, I'm sure she heard you."

"Yeah, we all heard you. It was pretty hard not to, what with all the screaming and what have you," Alec said with a laugh as he returned to the car so he could park it. But not before I flipped him off, which only made him laugh harder as he drove away.

Zayne's expression softened, his teasing demeanor fading. "Look, man, Bash was my brother. He loved that girl, and she loved him."

"And this conversation is fucking over."

"Listen, I'm not trying to mess with you. It's just…I've seen the way she looks at you, too. It might be a betrayal to him to say this, but he wanted her to be happy, so maybe you should both stop dancing around it."

"What is it with you and dancing metaphors?"

Zayne laughed, the sound light and genuine. "Hey, it gets the point across. Doesn't it? Besides, life's too short not to have a little fun with words."

I kept my guards firmly in place, but could see why Ezra liked this guy. "Look, kid, don't overcomplicate things.

She's my Luna. That's all. We're a pack at war. We can't afford those types of distractions."

"Yeah, no. I'm sure I overstepped, Alpha. I'm just saying, Ezra. She isn't just anybody."

No, she sure isn't.

"And…she's your Luna. If anyone is worth the risk, it's her."

With that, he turned and ran up the stairs, heading toward my dolly, and leaving me here to ponder my next moves.

Was I *falling* for her? The daughter of the man I had sworn to destroy? What a cruel twist of fate, a betrayal of my own heart if it were true. I had made a solemn vow—a promise etched into my very soul. Revenge had been my only purpose and driving force all these years. And yet, every time I looked at her, that purpose wavered.

I clenched my fists, frustration boiling within me. "What am I doing?" I muttered to myself, my voice barely above a whisper. "I can't let this happen. I won't let this happen."

Yet, the questions persisted, gnawing at the edges of my resolve, festering in my mind, like a damn parasite.

Was it right to hold Ezra accountable for the sins of her father? Did right or wrong ever have a role to play in this, or were the two destined to be forever entwined, shadows of one another?

Time was rapidly slipping away, and I knew I needed clarity —a way to reconcile the conflict between my emotions and my sworn duty. But her presence ignited such turmoil within me, causing me to question the very foundations upon which I had built my life. I attempted to distance myself from her, but the memory of her radiant smile, her inner strength, and her recklessness kept pulling me back, like a siren's call in the night.

I inhaled deeply, striving to regain my composure, to fortify the walls around my heart. Weakness was a luxury I couldn't afford, a vulnerability that threatened to shatter everything.

I pulled out my phone. My fingers hovering just above her name. I knew if I pushed her, I could twist the variables until she saw the truth I wanted her to see. Yet, the thought of her slipping away, of losing all the control I so desperately craved, sent a jolt of anger coursing through my veins. "No," I hissed, clenching my fists. "She will never have that power over me."

I shoved the phone back into my jeans, just in time for Alec to stroll up the walk behind me.

"June? You good, bro?"

"Yeah. I'm good. Come on. I want Ezra to be seen by the physician, and her cuts cleaned. See that it's done."

"Yeah, sure. I got it, but what about you?"

"I'm fine."

He pointed to my shirt, where the fabric was darkening as crimson seeped through, staining the cloth from the fresh claw marks against my stomach. *Well, shit. I liked this shirt.*

"How many?" Alec asked as we started up the stairs.

"Six. But I'm counting the big guy as two."

He chuckled, then with a much more serious tone asked, "You really killed their Beta?"

"He touched her."

"I see."

"What?" I questioned rather aggressively. "Spit it out, Alec. It's not like you to keep your thoughts to yourself."

"I'm just thinking, maybe the kid…had a good argument."

"He's wrong."

"Deny your feelings all you want, but we both know you're walking a dangerous line. It's only a matter of time, if you like her, before the whole plan begins to crumble."

"Again, with this? I don't like her. She's nothing but a toy to pass the time."

"Whatever you say…but remember, toys can break, and so can hearts," he said, fisting my shoulder as we continued up the stairs.

"She's stronger than people give her credit for. Reckless and headstrong, sure, but brave. Her heart will mend."

"She's got fight in her. And she survived the death of her mate. Nobody is questioning her strength. Though it isn't *her* heart I'm worried about. How long have we been friends?"

"All my life."

"Exactly. And in all that time, I've never seen you commit to anyone. There have been women, yes, but I doubt you'd slaughter six wolves for any of them."

He hit the nail on the head. I sure as hell wouldn't have gone to such lengths for any of the women I'd been with before her. I never intended for her to step foot inside that compound, but I'd held back initially, watching her toy with them, a fierce grace in her defiance. I was mesmerized.

She didn't portray an ounce of fear, even against that hulking brute who loomed over her like a specter. But when I witnessed his fist slam into her. Heard that sickening thud. Watched her body collapsing. Something inside me shattered.

This girl exasperated me more often than not. She constantly invaded my thoughts, challenging everything I believed.

I resented the way she burrowed under my skin, stirring emotions I thought I had long suppressed. She was supposed to be insignificant—merely a pawn.

And yet, for the first time since I was a child, I had no self-control. Composure was lost to me; I was careless, consumed by an uncontrollable rage. *I wanted those wolves dead.*

She was *mine*.

My little toy.

My dolly.

My Luna.

Fucking *mine*.

Why did I feel this overwhelming possessiveness? And why, by the Goddess, did she make me question and second-guess every decision? How the hell had I become so...vulnerable?

I didn't need this distraction. Not now. Not ever. But there she was, a storm in my life, unraveling me piece by piece, and there wasn't a damn thing I could do to stop it.

Did I even want to?

As the night droned on, the questions kept surfacing. The need to settle my mind, growing near unbearable. I felt no remorse for the scouts' impending demise, yet her ingratitude stirred a restless disquiet within me. Of all the reasons Ezra could detest me, this one was inexplicable; I had, after all, saved her damn life. She doesn't get to be angry at me for that.

I was pacing back and forth, this pain growing in my temple, sharp, piercing, menacing. Before I could comprehend what I was doing, I was moving toward her on autopilot. I couldn't leave it alone. I hated the way we had left things. The entire ride home, all we did was argue. She never even looked in my direction, but once.

She had put herself in unnecessary danger with no real plan and no backup; if I hadn't installed those security cameras outside her windows and at her bedroom door, she'd be lost to me now.

I had somewhat regretted the cameras up until now. Don't get me wrong; information is power…usually. But Zayne was often posted outside her bedroom door, and I had received one too many notifications from the surveillance camera feed, which showed him narrating his patrol, as if he were the main character in an action film, complete with sound effects. I've also seen him try to balance all kinds of things on his head, unsuccessfully.

One time, I recall him having a full-blown conversation with what might've been a bug, which he had named Atlas. And yes, Atlas came complete with a voice and personality of his own.

I had thought briefly about moving that camera inside her room, but quickly brushed that thought aside.

That invasion of her privacy, as protective as I might be about this girl, was a line, even I wouldn't cross.

Still, I would never have known she left. I wouldn't have been able to find her or bring her home if I hadn't thought ahead so that I could better control situations like these.

Ufffgh. Home.

I couldn't even remember what having a home felt like. So, when did I begin thinking of Night Tree's pack house as home?

When I opened her door, she was sitting on the edge of her bed, facing the farthest wall, crying. Her head snapped in my direction, and she wiped fresh tears onto the sleeves of her old hoodie.

Fucking crying again. This girl is killing me.

I walked inside, my hands instinctively reaching in her direction like I was going to…what? Hold her? Tell her everything was gonna be okay?

She stood up, moving around the bed with her arm outstretched like a stop sign, causing me to freeze where I stood. "No. Don't you dare touch me."

I couldn't help but be in awe of the sight of her. She was wearing an oversized hoodie, but her legs were completely exposed.

Those fucking legs, shit.

It wasn't the place that made the pack house home…it was *her*.

CHAPTER TWELVE

Fucking Hurt Me

Juno's POV

My jeans suddenly felt too tight as I felt my cock growing in length, sliding down along my inner thigh, throbbing at the sight of her.

"Get the fuck out!" she shrieked, pointing to the door.

Raising my brows, I cocked my head to the side. I don't know what I was expecting. I knew she was pissed off. Crying? While unnerving, it didn't surprise me. She did that often. But pissed off to the point of crying? That I was trying not to find amusing. I might've come here to check on her, but those weren't tears of sorrow, and she had no fucks to give right now.

When she tore those eyes away, the pride and lust swelling in me vanished. *You were being so strong, little one. Don't step down now. Not to me. Not to anyone.*

"Look at me…" I demanded, but she didn't. She just moved past me to the door.

I repeated myself, this time a bit louder. "I said…Look. At. Me."

"Go to hell," she countered, still refusing to look my way, "I. Said. Get the *fuck* out," she snapped again, the words grinding between her teeth as she reached to open the door.

"Ezra, look at me!" I said, slamming it shut as quickly as she attempted to open it. Finally, her eyes shot to my face, and I softened. "I know you probably hate me and might even think I'm a monster, but please let me explain."

"Oh, Juno, I don't think it. I fucking know," she said, her eyes still blazing. And it was a beautiful sight, just fucking *beautiful.*

"You might have thought there was a choice, but there was never one. Not for me. You are my Luna, and I have a duty, as did they, to ensure your safety."

"And who was ensuring their safety?" she challenged.

"The scouts should have absconded, but people are going to die. That's a fact." She was delusional if she thought this would be anything beyond what it was. This is war. The harsh reality of it has inevitable consequences.

Death and chaos were knocking at our doorstep, and I would not allow her to be a casualty. If anyone was going to destroy this girl, it was going to be me. If she needed me to be the one to give her the hard truths, so be it.

"Is that all, Alpha?" she asked, her voice brimming with annoyance and defiance.

My eyes narrowed and flickered again with amusement. "No, little toy." My tone was low and commanding. "Take it off," I said, eyeing the only piece of clothing on her body. *Was she wearing panties?* Curiosity killed the cat and marred the pup, but my wolf needed to know.

"Excuse me?" she asked, confused or stunned by the shift in conversation. Make no mistake. I couldn't suffer this need or want anymore, and I was going to take her, willing or not.

Ezra's heart was beating rapidly in her chest, but she stood her ground, ready to rechallenge me, intensifying my wolf's hunger. I could see the determination in her eyes, daring me to make a move.

"Enough of these games!" my wolf Kai roared.

"Agreed."

I reached behind her head, gathering her hair in a tangled mess at the base of her neck, and pulled down, exposing her neck to me. I leaned down and repeated into her ear in a throaty, rumbling growl that rolled out slowly. "I said, take it off, dolly."

She attempted to pull away, and I quickly halted the movement, pulling down harder on her hair. My hand on her hip turned and pushed her up against the door forcefully, the impact of her body echoing through the room. I pushed my body into hers, and she gasped. The whimper that followed had my jaw clenching.

As I looked at the object of my unfiltered desire, a feverish, almost maddening obsession took over. My thoughts were spinning out of control, each one more relentless and demanding than the last. I no longer cared about the implications; I wanted her.

"I would traverse the darkest depths, face the fiercest storms, and break every goddamn rule to keep you safe, dolly. Hate me for my choice. But you remain unharmed, and I, with a clear conscience."

Her eyes widened as I exposed my canines, dragging them along the subtle contours of her neck, delicate and smooth, like fine silk draped over a porcelain frame. When I felt her hands move along my sides, I growled again…hoarse and raspy, like claws scraping over stone, revealing the desperate need to taste every facet of this woman.

I bent slightly, lifting her effortlessly at the waist, her feet dangling in the air as I hoisted her over my shoulder. She gasped, her hands instinctively resting on my back to steady herself as I spun around. There was a blur of motion as I carried her with a determined stride to the bed, tossing her down onto it.

She didn't fight against the movement, and once she hit, she wiggled the bottom of the hoodie up from under her ass. Shimmying it up over her head, revealing her body to me.

"Good girl, dolly," I praised as I looked over her body's symphony of curves and lines. Her silhouetted body, outlined by nothing more than the glow of the silver moon shining through the windows, was truly a masterful sight. I mean, this girl was perfect.

Her skin was glowing, reflecting the moon's rays and revealing what might be the very essence of vitality and life. She leaned back, resting on her elbows. Her breasts were swollen with a fullness that pleased my wolf. Those perfect breasts were exposed to me in the most vulnerable way.

I moved to the long dresser against the wall and opened the top left drawer. The room still whispered the essence of her lost mate, and I found that frustrating.

His helmet still rested on a shelf, its visor reflecting the soft glow of the nearby lamp. Two biker jackets hung on a rack next to the dresser. I doubt the abandoned gaming setup belonged to my girl. Yet, her touch was evident throughout the room. A soft, blue-hued throw blanket was draped over the bed, its fabric inviting and warm.

A framed photograph of them sat on the dresser. I flipped it down and pulled out two pairs of pantyhose. I also knew she had no restraints in her room, which pleased me in a sense. This was something I could give her that he hadn't.

"What are you…?" Her voice trailed off as she watched me. "Juno? How did you know that was my panty drawer?" I didn't answer as I pushed the drawer shut, returning to the edge of the bed and kneeling on it in front of her.

"How did you know I left the pack house?"

So many questions.

"Ufffgh." The soft, dismissive sound escaped my lips as I looked down at her.

"Juno! How did you know?" she demanded again.

I dropped the pantyhose down beside her, grabbed her black, lace panties, and ripped them off her body. She leaned up and smacked me hard across the face. "Fucking answer me!" she shouted.

Good. She's mad. I like it better when she fights back.

"That's all you got, dolly?" I taunted, a smug grin spreading across my face.

Her eyes narrowed, and she shot back, "You arrogant prick. Answer the fucking question." A determined fire lit up her expression, matching the challenge in her voice as she smacked me again.

"Quit acting like a little bitch, and fucking hurt me," I snapped. "Or roll over and get fucked like one."

She wrapped her legs around my waist, locking her ankles, and rolled over, forcing me to lose my footing. As I hit the bed, she shifted so that she now sat on top of me, her smooth, wet pussy pressing against my stomach. I planted my feet on the ground to steady myself, my ass barely on the bed. She pulled her fist back and punched me square in the jaw.

"Good girl, you're learning," I said as I ran my thumb over the split in my lip, wiping the blood away with a proud grin. I grabbed her wrists and moved them to her ankles.

"Hold, and don't fucking move," I demanded, grabbing the pantyhose and securing her left wrist to her ankle. Her right hand moved up my chest, tracing the ridges of my muscles through my shirt with her fingers. *Fucking brat.*

She wrapped her hand around my throat and leaned forward, her weight bearing down on my throat. "Speak," she hissed. "Have you been going through my things?"

Several fucking times, dolly. But you don't need to know that.

I wrapped my arms under her thighs and planted my hands firmly around her ass, picking her up. She yelped, clearly not expecting this. Pushing her forward so that her slick, glistening pussy was hovering over my face, I traced my tongue along the folds of her perfect pussy, before sucking that swollen bud into my mouth.

She moaned involuntarily and tried to crawl forward, but her restrained leg caused her to fall onto her face.

I turned over and grabbed her hips, pulling her body back so that her ass was pressed against me, grabbed her right wrist, and secured it to her right ankle.

I leaned forward over her body and wrapped my hand around her throat, lifting her face, "You might think you have some power here, but you don't. You are mine. I own you," I said before I shoved her face into the bed and smacked her ass. A loud crack was drowned out by her moan of pleasure.

"Fuck, look at you. I'm gonna own this fucking ass tonight, too," I promised, unlatching my belt.

"Touch my ass and die," she countered.

"I warned you that your dirty mouth would get you into trouble one of these days." I laughed.

I gave her another hard smack. Her cheek began to flush almost immediately, a deep crimson spreading outward in the shape of my hand.

I stood up, dropping my pants to the floor and kicking them off. She turned her face, and her eyes immediately landed on my cock as I walked around the bed, stroking it. Looking down at her, I reached down, lifting her by her throat, and shoved my cock into her mouth.

"I'm gonna wash that dirty fucking mouth out, and when I'm done, you won't be able to say another goddamn word."

I was gonna destroy that filthy mouth. I wasted no time. I could feel myself pushing into her throat. And a growl rumbled deep in my chest, like the distant thunder of an approaching storm. Plunging into her until I was balls deep. She gagged, and tears ran down the curve of her cheek. I pulled out, allowing her to take a deep breath, then shoved myself back in; her gagging and choking, mixed with those slutty whimpers, had me ravenous.

I fisted my hands in her hair as I grabbed her head with both hands and fucked her, hard and deep. Her saliva mixed with my pre-cum was seeping out around my cock and down her chin in foamy bubbles. Tears glistened in the corners of her eyes as she choked on every inch of me. Her eyes rolled back as I deprived her of everything but my cock, and looking down at her that way pushed me over the edge.

I could feel my release approaching, my balls swelling, the pressure building in my core. The sensation was one I'd never experienced before. It's not like I've never cum before. But this felt like every nerve cell in my brain was firing all at once, and it was all-consuming.

I was slipping away into an ethereal plane. And she was about to feel my soul leaving my body, my shaft began to pulse and tingle. I wouldn't last any longer when she looked and felt this good. And damn, did her mouth feel good.

I pulled out for a second, allowing her a breath, "Swallow every fucking drop, dolly," I said as I thrust deep into her throat and let go, a massive stream of thick cum shooting down it. The swallowing suction of her throat as she took it all so beautifully sent a soul-crushing shudder through my body as she milked every last drop with that glorious motion.

"Good fucking girl," I said, pulling my cock out and smacking it against her cheek. She was panting, breathing heavily, and her face was covered in a mix of snot, spit, and foam, but that smack made a satisfying smile curve on her lips as she wiped her face on the bed and looked up at me. And I swear, after that orgasm, I went temporarily brain-dead, cause this mess of a woman was the absolute best sight I'd ever laid my eyes on.

I leaned down, pinching her cheeks in my hand, and slid my tongue between those full lips. The taste of me lingered there as she welcomed the kiss, deepening it. *Shit.*

Shit. Shit. What in the actual fuck was I doing? Pushing all this gay shit aside.

I rolled her over, grabbing the nylon restraints and pushing her hips, spinning her around so that I could see her beautiful, soaked pussy.

"So fucking wet," I said, pushing her thighs apart even further. She was already restrained in a way that revealed herself to me, but I wanted to enjoy the view to the fullest. I ran my fingers from her dripping opening to her clit, swirling the smooth wetness around it.

She let out a moan.

I curved two fingers into her pussy, thrusting upwards as I leaned down, swirling my tongue around her swollen bud. Drawing it into my mouth and suckling on it caused her to moan again. Fuck, if the way she sounded couldn't stir the very depths of my soul, then nothing ever could.

"Yes!" she cried out, clearly reveling in that motion.

I released her clit and looked up at her. "Who am I?" I asked as I started thrusting my fingers faster and deeper into her center. The way her hips were moving told me she was getting close to her release now, so I used my other hand to pinch and circle her clit for good measure.

"WHO AM I?" I said again.

"Fuuuuck," she groaned, still not answering me.

I reached up and wrapped my hand around her throat. "I said, who the fuck am I, dolly?"

"My husband." She tried to yell, but my hand around her throat wouldn't allow it. It came out as a barely audible whisper, cracked and hoarse after the beating her mouth had just taken.

"That's right, and you are MINE. Now let it go for me, dolly," I commanded.

Her eyes rolled back as her chin lifted, her body trembled beneath me as she released her essence all over my fingers. I didn't stop. I wanted more. I began circling my thumb over that sensitive, swollen clit, while I swirled my fingers inside her.

She tried to close her legs, but the restraints prevented it. She began rolling her hips from side to side and trying desperately to escape the overstimulation of her clit, before she started both laughing and crying out, the pain and pleasure mixing into another beautiful sound from her lips, a melody that resonated deeply.

"Please, stop," she begged. But she needed to know who was in control here. Me. I was in control. She was my little toy, my dolly, my Luna, fucking all of it, and she belonged to me.

"Relax, little toy," I whispered as I removed my fingers, slid them into her mouth, hooked her cheek, and lifted her face to mine.

"I OWN YOU," I said as I thrust my cock into her dripping pussy. She inhaled sharply and let out a raspy cry. I could feel her tightening around my cock, and I increased my thrusts.

"Say it, dolly," I commanded. She shook her head disobediently. So, I smacked her to remind her who was in charge, and she let out a startled breath.

"Say. It."

She whimpered quietly as she shook her head again. I pulled out just enough to allow rotation as I flipped her over to her knees again; she was five foot something, short-as-shit and had no weight to her, so it wasn't a challenging task. Lifting her hips and driving myself into her again, I pulled her into me while I plunged forward in slow, hard thrusts.

With each drive, she let out a soft cry. "Who? Owns? You?" I asked again between thrusts.

"Fuck, you do!" Her voice cracked, quickly replaced with a deep, guttural moan.

I pulled out of her sweet pussy and fucked her with my fingers until she soaked my hand; she was dripping down her thighs and onto the bed. I scooped it up and rubbed it over her tight anus. Her eyes darted back to me. "No," she warned.

A smile curling on my lips, I shoved my finger in her ass, massaging it and stretching it out, before adding another.

"Please, don't! Stop," she moaned. I'm not sure she was convinced she didn't want this anymore.

I grabbed her tit with my other hand and whispered. "I. Own. You. All of you. And this is my ass. Now, breath, dolly, this is gonna hurt."

I shoved my cock into her ass. A gentleman would have gone slow, but she didn't need that; she needed the pain and the pleasure that only I could give her.

She was a freak, her presence fierce and enchanting. She was a living embodiment of untamed beauty and raw power—a fiery, red-haired goddess who commanded my movements.

She cried out in pain. I reached down and smacked her pussy before rubbing her clit as I began thrusting slowly in and out. Her painful cries were soon replaced with moans of pleasure, and I picked up speed. *That's right, dolly. You know you love it.*

THWACK.

The sound of my hand on her ass left her choking on soft whimpers, accompanied by huffed-out moans of pleasure. Setting my soul ablaze. With a deep, guttural grunt and one final thrust, I released myself, filling her sweet ass.

"Such a good fucking girl," I breathed, pulling out and squeezing the excess cum out onto her back.

I left her there while I went to her bathroom. I turned on the bathwater and tested it, ensuring it was at an adequate temperature. Although I'm sure she was one of those psychopaths who wanted their bath water ushered in straight from the pits of hell, I decided on a less *blistering your skin, and melting your flesh from your bones*, warmth. I grabbed a towel out of the closet and returned to her.

"Get me the fuck out of these," she said, but I couldn't help myself. I wanted to look at the masterpiece before me.

Cum was leaking out of her ass, running down the folds of her pussy, and there was a large spot between her knees, soaked on the bed.

"Juno?!" she yelled, slightly annoyed.

"Yes, little toy?" I questioned, still taking in the view.

"NOW."

"Oh, you want it done now? Well, aren't we demanding? Maybe I'll get to it…if I feel like it," I said, folding my hands over my chest.

"This isn't funny, untie me," she whined.

"Well, since you asked so nicely…I might consider it."

"Juno!" she yelled again, angrily.

I smirked and leaned closer. "Well, well, someone's in quite the predicament. What's the magic word?"

"Get me the fuck out of these or I'm gonna beat your ass!"

I chuckled softly. "Okay, hold still," I said, reaching down and beginning to untie the makeshift restraints. "The secret word was 'please,' by the way, but since you're in a bind, I'll let it slide this time."

"Funny," she said, unamused.

I made a mental note that pantyhose work really well as restraints. I might have to invest in some more and a gag. Once she was free, her legs stretched out, and I might have felt bad, but the look on her face told me she was more than satisfied.

"Still mad at me?"

"Yes…Maybe," she said as I picked her up and carried her to the bathroom.

"Let's get you cleaned up, little one," I said, dipping her into the bath and lathering her body with coconut-scented body wash.

After a long pause, she looked up at me. "Why are you doing this?"

I tapped her leg, and she lifted it so I could run the soapy loofa down it, being sure to scrub every inch down to her toes. Then I lowered her leg into the water and tapped her other leg. She lifted it, allowing me to repeat the motion. Once I had scrubbed her entire body, I poured water over her hair, and she tilted her head back.

I lathered her hair and rinsed it. Soapy bubbles swirled and danced on the water's surface, mimicking the thoughts racing through my mind. I really wasn't sure why I was doing this. As much as I enjoyed hurting her, I also wanted to take care of her.

Without a word, I pulled her out of the bath and wrapped her in a towel. She hooked the towel around her body and reached up for the towel hanging to the side, scrunching her curls to dry them. They fell in loose, wet ringlets around her shoulders.

I sighed and gently pulled the plug from the drain. The water began to swirl away, taking the last of the bubbles with it.

"Get dressed, dolly. You're sleeping in my room tonight." My tone left no room for argument. She nodded. And I went to the window while she dressed, peeking out into the night.

CHAPTER THIRTEEN

We Fucked, That's All.

Now Drop It.

Ezra's POV

Tomorrow marks five weeks since I lost Bash, and it's been a week since we've heard from Gabe, since that phone call, and my insane plan to save the scouts—which admittedly did not go according to plan. I never did make it inside the barracks, and Juno had killed Thomas, so we've been stuck waiting and preparing for the fallout.

Junior has kicked the pack's training into overdrive, even though on the war front there has been complete radio silence. Things were becoming stable, almost comfortable, as I fought to keep up with the new training schedule.

I wish I could say that silence gave me peace of mind, but instead, it left me drowning in a river of anxious thoughts and sleepless nights. I was having nightmares of Bash and waking up every morning dealing with the aftermath of it all, which left me feeling both mentally and physically drained.

We still haven't heard a word from the scouts. Suffice it to say, they were likely killed long ago, like Juno had said. My pleas to reach out on their behalf were quickly silenced by *his fucking majesty*. The guilt rested in the corners of my mind with all the rest now. Junior had attempted to save me from that guilt by putting the nail in their coffins himself, but the weight rested on my shoulders all the same.

Today's training session has been incredibly long. The golden light from the setting sun mocked my already aching muscles. The light cast long shadows across the training grounds, dancing like specters on the worn snow-covered Earth. We'd been running drills for hours, and Junior now stood with a gaze as sharp as his blade at the center, his presence commanding respect and attention.

"Alright, everyone, form up!" Junior's clear and authoritative voice rang out. The trainees, a mix of seasoned fighters and eager novices, quickly assembled into a rough semicircle. I stood among them, tired but determined.

The drills were repetitive and designed to hone our reflexes and sharpen our skills. I've learned to move with a newfound grace in the last few weeks. Unlike him, I would never be a Warrior, but I could at least hold my own now.

My movements have become more fluid and precise, and my emotions…less overwhelming. I've been training tirelessly, staying late to practice with Zayne, and running extra laps. Today, I was pleasantly surprised by my progress. The additional work seemed to be paying off.

Outside of these daily training sessions, I had barely seen Juno. He had been making it a point to avoid me. So, I was startled when he called out, "Ezra, you're up." Wearing that cocky, all-knowing smile of his.

The way his voice wrapped around my name had left a gentle storm brewing in my chest. It was like hearing a forgotten melody, both sweet and haunting. Stirring emotions, I had thought, were now safely tucked away since our last night together.

Wrapping those emotions up tightly and forcing them to the back of my mind, I raised an eyebrow. I offered him a little smirk as I stepped forward without hesitation.

"Show me what you've got," he instructed, taking a fighting stance.

There might have been a hint of defiance in my otherwise steady voice as I responded, "Gladly."

I took a deep breath to calm myself and entered my fighting position. I was still annoyed with him for avoiding me, but I wouldn't let him see the effect he had on me.

I watched his every movement and was ready for him when he lunged at me. His strikes were swift and calculated, but I parried his blows with deft movements, my petite frame aiding my agile footwork. Something

Zayne has been helping me with. He stood tall, pride evident in his stance, watching from the sidelines.

"Good Job, dolly," Junior praised, a rare, genuine smile touching his lips. "But remember, always stay on the balls of your feet. It gives you better balance and quicker reactions."

I nodded, absorbing his advice like a sponge, and adjusted my stance. Fucking dick was always right, and I felt the difference immediately.

"Better," he said, wasting no time before launching another series of attacks. This time, he was much more aggressive; as his arm shot out, I ducked and swept my leg under him. He jumped and spun around, landing a kick to my stomach. I would have fallen back right on my ass, but his hand around my wrist kept me upright. I don't know how he moved so quickly, but I could feel the aggravation growing.

There was no way in hell I would let him make a fool of me a second time. A lot has changed since the last time we sparred in front of the pack. I ripped my wrist out of his hand, and he chuckled. "Calm yourself, little one," he taunted.

"Oh, I'm calm. Is that all you've got?" I shot back, getting back into my stance.

"No, we're done," he said, turning away. "You should be proud. You did well."

I squared my shoulders. "We are far from done," I said, lunging forward. He somehow managed to block and counterattack even with his back to me, but I met him head-on. I could feel my confidence growing as our weapons locked together, neither of us willing to give an inch.

"You've been avoiding me," I said, hushed so only he could hear me. "Why?"

My chest heaved with the exertion, but I held my ground.

"No. I haven't," he replied. He wasn't even breaking a sweat.

"Fucking bullshit, you can fool everyone else here, but I know you, and I know something is bothering you."

"You know nothing," he said, losing his edge.

Whispers and murmurs swirled around us like a restless wind, but I stood firm, unyielding. Every eye was fixed on us, the intensity of their stares pressed down on me, a reminder of the stakes and a source of silent support. "I know you miss me," I teased.

He exhaled sharply, trying to hold back his amusement, but it gave me the needed opening. I pushed him back, attacking again, and ensured that I kept my weight forward. My strikes were no longer hesitant, but purposeful and powerful. I moved with a dancer's grace and a seasoned warrior's precision.

Junior finally stepped back after what felt like an eternity, lowering his weapon. "That's enough for today," he announced, then addressed our pack.

"I hope you were all paying attention. The battle isn't always limited to physical strength; tactics and wit can tip the scales in your favor."

I stepped back, putting my sword on the weapons rack. Zayne immediately pulled me into his arms, and my heart swelled with pride.

"You were amazing, Ezra!" he gushed as many other pack members swarmed around me. I shook hands and thanked them as they all told me how great I had been. They seemed proud to call me their Luna at that moment. I had always felt like Luna was an undeserved title. While I was proud of my pack, I never truly felt accepted until now. When Dalton emerged from the crowd to congratulate me, the joy he brought with him was infectious.

"You've really come a long way from the uncertain fighter you once were," he said, bowing before me as if I were royalty, "and if you desire a crown, you've most certainly earned it."

I snorted, a gut-wrenching laugh escaping me as I allowed him to take my hand. "I've never wanted the crown, Dalton."

"And yet, it fits. Like Cinderella's glass slipper," he joked, taking my hand and placing a kiss on the top of it.

"I'm no Cinderella," I said, shaking my head at this crazy Gamma and peaking over his bowed position to where Juno had just stood. He was gone, and it took me a minute to shake that unexpected sadness away before I turned my attention back to Dalton and Zayne.

"No, you are not, but you've made me and your pack proud today," he assured me.

"Thank you," I said sincerely, smiling at the Gamma before me. "Please, excuse me."

Zayne fell into step beside me as the sun dipped below the horizon, casting a warm glow over the training grounds.

"Where you go, I go." He shrugged, and I pulled him along, making my way to Junior's office. As much as I had been trying to convince myself that I hated him, something with us had definitely shifted.

Maybe it was the way he had made a claim over me, or perhaps it was the soul-crushing way he fucked me that was leading me to him. But how he cared for me after, and the avoidance for the past week, had left me confused and wanting answers. His touch had been firm yet tender after, and his absence now felt like a gaping wound, leaving me adrift in a sea of uncertainty.

Juno and Alec were locked in an intense argument when I entered the office.

"By all means, don't let me interrupt," I joked as they both fell silent.

"Luna," Alec said, bowing his head in my direction.

"Are you gonna tell me what's happening, or is that above my pay grade?" I asked half-heartedly.

When the door opened behind me, Junior and Alec both turned their attention to the girl standing in the doorway.

"We'll finish this chat later," Alec said, moving past me and messing up the girl's hair before walking out the door.

"Nyx, hey…just the girl I wanted to see," Junior greeted her.

"Nyx?" I asked, confused, but I'd seen this girl before. She was the same bitch who gave Kit a hard time in the hallway before. What was she doing here?

"The one and only," she said, moving past me and hugging Junior tightly, which he definitely reciprocated. That same devilish smirk was playing on her lips as before as she looked over his shoulder at me.

"Luna, meet Nyx. Nyx is an admirable warrior and a long-time friend of mine."

"Nice to meet you, Nyx," I greeted her, somewhat hesitantly.

"Luna, if you could excuse us, I have some things to discuss with Nyx," he said suddenly, and I couldn't believe it.

"Oh, is that so?" I asked, turning my attention to Juno.

"It's nothing for you to worry your pretty little head about," he responded.

"You forget, this is my pack, too."

"Ezra, please. I'm quite busy at the moment."

"It's okay, I'll come back later," Nyx said, brushing her hand against his shoulder in a way that made me uneasy before making her way out of the room.

Juno sat back in his chair, crossing his arms across his chest and looking at me with a shade of annoyance.

"A friend?" I questioned him once she was gone. I knew I had no right to question him, and yet…there was something about this girl I didn't trust. I couldn't help it. The words slipped out against my better judgment.

He didn't answer, so I moved around the desk, lifting his face with two fingers as I sat on the desk before him, leaning down so his gaze met mine.

"Can we please talk?" I asked, searching his eyes.

"About?"

"Juno, what happened between us? It was…"

"A mistake," he finished for me.

"Is that how you truly feel? Can you honestly sit here and tell me that what happened was a mistake? Which fucking time?" I pushed; I didn't believe him. Despite everything, there was so much more to him than what he wanted anyone to see.

"Yes. That's how I feel." His voice was even, but I softened as I searched his eyes. He wasn't telling me the truth.

"Why are you pushing me away? I can see it in your eyes. There's something you aren't telling me. Is it her? Is it because of Nyx?"

Juno's jaw tightened, his hands clenching and unclenching at his sides. "There's nothing for us to talk about. I owe you nothing. We fucked, that's all. Now drop it."

I stood up, cradling his head between my hands, refusing to relinquish without a fight. I meant something to him. I had to. He wouldn't have avoided me, this conversation, and his feelings if they didn't exist. And for a moment, he leaned into my touch.

Juno's POV

As she cradled my head, a rush of conflicting emotions rushed over me like waves against a rocky shore. The warmth of her touch sent shivers down my spine and ignited a spark of something I'd worked so hard to bury deep within.

The memories came flooding back—the promises I made, the vengeance I swore. But in her gentle embrace, there was a flicker of solace, a reminder of the humanity I thought had been lost.

With a heavy sigh, I closed my eyes tight, allowing myself just a moment of vulnerability. This woman was either going to save me or shatter everything I'd fought for. Her gentle voice pulled me out of that moment.

"I can't just drop it. I care about you, and I think you care about me, too. Why can't you just admit it?"

Ezra's POV

His eyes flashed with anger, a storm brewing within him. "This isn't some damn fairy tale where things just work out, princess. It's so much more complicated than that."

"It's complicated?" I echoed, my frustration bubbling over. "What's so complicated about saying how you fucking feel? Why can't you just be honest?"

His patience snapped. "Just STOP! STOP asking so many fucking questions."

"Juno, I—"

He cut me off, pushing his chair back with a forceful kick, rising to his feet, and positioning himself so close that I could feel his breath mingling with mine.

"You just keep pushing and pushing, leave it the fuck alone. Stop trying to fix everything."

Tears began to well up and sting my eyes. If I still had a heart, this might've broken it. It's not that I expected him to love me; I didn't even like him ninety percent of the time, but I thought I meant something. At the very least, I didn't deserve this. "I'm not trying to fix anything. I just wanted to be there for you. I wanted to face this war with you."

The fury that once burned hot within him had transformed into a chilling determination. Every emotion, every ounce of rage, was now a weapon, honed and sharpened, ready to be wielded with precision. His eyes, once ablaze with fury, now gleamed with a steely, unwavering focus. "Well, I can't have you in this fucking war. Alec and I will manage it. It's better if you just stay out of my damn way."

The words hung in the air between us, a bitter finality to them. I came here for answers. And I forced him to give them to me.

Every bit of pain I felt was my own doing. It was my fault, my own foolish mistake, for believing this was more than it ever could be.

"Fine. If that's what you want," I whispered as I moved his arm and pushed past him.

"Ezra..." He said my name, and it felt like a plea leaving his mouth. I had to blink back the tears.

"Don't. I wanted to know where we stood. What I was to you. I wasn't quite prepared for the truth of it, but you already told me, even if I didn't want to hear it. I'm just your little toy, right?"

"I will fucking break you."

"You will never break me. But whether you accept it or not, I'm not going anywhere, you selfish fucking prick. This is my pack, too."

"Selfish? I'm fucking selfish?"

"Yes, Juno. This is OUR damned burden. Yours and mine, to face together."

His eyes narrowed. "You think me protecting you is selfish?" His voice was a low, menacing growl.

I held my ground, my heart pounding, and my resolve unwavering. "I don't think. I know. This pack is mine just as much as it's yours. And I will not be sidelined in this fight. You don't have to care about me or even like me, but you are stuck with me."

Silence hung in the air for a moment, the tension almost unbearable. Without another word, I turned on my heel and stormed out, leaving him standing there alone. The weight of our confrontation still pressing down on me, I slammed the door, flipping him off through it, and punched my fist through the wall.

Well, shit.

I pulled out my phone and searched my contacts until I found Flynn's name. She was in Gabe's pack, but she had always been a good friend to me. I took a deep breath and hit call.

The line rang out, and I almost hung up until there was a small click on the other end.

"Ezra?" Her voice was hushed. "One second."

Through the phone, I caught the faint rustling of fabric as she moved, the soft creak of a door easing open. Her footsteps were hesitant and light, padding across the floor, each one a whisper against the silence.

There was a brief pause, the sound of breath held in anticipation, followed by the faint click of a door closing behind her.

"Ezzie? Are you still there?" she asked, breaking through the hushed stillness, followed by the steady rhythm of her breathing.

"Flynn, I've missed you so much," I said into the phone.

"It's really you? You shouldn't be calling me. If Gabe finds out..."

"Are you okay?" I asked. Her fear of him made my heart ache sickly. I had been afraid of him, too; I knew what that felt like.

"I'm…okay, Ez. It's not me I'm worried about. He wants you back."

"What's his plan?" I hesitated to ask, knowing what she would be risking if she answered, but I needed to know.

"Ez. I don't have much time. Here is what I know. Gabe knows that brute force won't be enough to get you back. He's been biding his time, gathering intel on your pack's weaknesses."

That makes sense; that was our first move, too. Knowledge is power.

"His plan, as far as I can tell, is to create a diversion, something big enough to draw your new husband's attention away from you."

"He's gonna attack the border," I thought out loud.

"I don't know," she answered, although it wasn't a question. That's what I would do: attack away from the main pack house and use that chaos to invade it.

"I do. That's what I would do," I said, quickly adding, "Flynn, stay safe. Okay. I love you. And…thank you."

"I love you, too. I'm sorry, I would have stayed with you, but my family…"

"I know, it's okay."

"I have to go. One month, maybe less," she said.

Click.

Chapter Fourteen

Un-Fucking-Believable, This Guy.

Juno's POV

I watched her walk away, and I could feel my heart aching with the weight of my unspoken feelings. I wasn't supposed to fall for her. But she was all I could think about, and that scared the fuck out of me.

Truth be told, there was absolutely nothing going on between me and Nyx; maybe it was wrong to let Ezra believe it was more than it was. But I could accept her hating me for that, the truth…the truth would be much more damaging.

The night had swallowed up both of us; the only thing left in this empty room was hurt and regret. I moved to the window, peeking out into the night. When I saw movement in the bushes, I quickly made my way to the hall. Ezra was just outside the door. "Go to my room," I ordered. "Lock the door and don't open it for anyone but me. Understand?"

"What?"

"Just do it."

"*Fine*. For fuck's sake, Juno."

I grabbed my phone and dialed Alec as I moved quickly down the hall. "Someone's outside."

"How many?"

"I'm not sure."

"On my way."

I hung up and called Zayne. "Ezra is in my room. Guard the door. Go there now."

"Everything okay?" he asked.

"Just do it." I hit *end call* and picked up my pace.

"*Hungry, Kai?*" I asked my wolf.

"*Ravenous.*"

"*Good. Get ready.*"

"*I'm always ready for blood.*"

Ezra's POV

I was pacing back and forth in Juno's room. Something in his tone made me retreat here without question. But as the minutes passed, I found myself growing impatient. Frustration and curiosity threatened to drive me to insanity.

What in the hell was going on?

Flynn had said one month, maybe sooner. But I had this nagging feeling after our conversation. Juno's demand for me to stay locked in this room hung over me like a shadow lurking just out of sight, whispering dread into my thoughts.

A tight knot in my stomach, this constant, uneasy flutter that wouldn't let me breathe, had my mind racing with all the dark possibilities. Every sound, every movement, felt like a harbinger of doom.

Something terrible was unfolding, and I couldn't escape its grip. I should be there; I'm Luna of this damn pack.

"I will not be caged!" Lana was growing even more impatient as I paced the room.

Unable to contain myself or my wolf for a second longer, I approached the door. I pressed my ear to it and heard nothing. Satisfied by the lack of movement in the halls, I turned the doorknob, cracking the door open, but when it opened wider, Zayne stepped into the opening.

"Fuck, Zayne, you scared the shit out of me!" I yelled, placing my hand over my now racing heart.

"Sorry, Ezra. I'm under orders to keep you in there."

"What the fuck? Juno's orders? And why is that?"

"I...I don't know," he said, scanning the halls before turning back to me. "I was just told to guard the door."

"Oh? Is that it?" I questioned.

"Yeaaah?" he answered slowly.

"Oh, good, you guard the door. I'll be going that way." I pointed down the hall.

"Ezra," he warned. "Don't make me force you back in there, please."

"Last I checked, you were my Gamma, meaning you are under a vow to protect and serve me." I was smiling because I knew he couldn't argue that fact.

He wasn't, because he knew I was right.

I shouldn't use his vow against him, but I've spent my whole life locked away, so one way or another, I was leaving this room.

"Dammit, Ezra."

"You can guard this door if you want, but I won't be hidden behind it," I said, ducking under his arm and heading down the hall. He was right there with me, just as I knew he would be.

The closer we got to the entrance, the louder the craziness outside became. Something had happened, and it wasn't good. Zayne and I glanced at each other, concern highlighting our brows. I took off running in an attempt to get there faster, but Zayne, still keeping pace with me, ordered me to wait.

He opened the front door of the pack house, stepped out, and motioned with his hand for me to stay put.

"*We fight!*" Lana snarled.

"*We fight,*" I confirmed, stepping through the door.

The scene that greeted me was chaos incarnate. Scouts, maybe? The Silver pack members clashed violently with Juno and his Beta. Fists were flying, and snarls echoed through the night. My eyes widened in shock; my breathing caught in my throat. I had just walked into a mindfuck, but my presence didn't go unnoticed.

One of the scouts lunged at me, and I dodged, my instincts kicking in slightly. Alec, seeing me in danger, delivered a decisive blow to the side of his head, sending him sprawling onto the ground. Zayne quickly pulled me backward, shielding my body with his own.

Well, shit.

Now, not only were they fighting, but their focus was on keeping me alive.

Juno, locked in a fierce struggle with another scout, shouted over the commotion, "Ezra, get the fuck inside, NOW!"

I should've listened. But I couldn't just do nothing. I sprinted forward, grabbing a nearby knife I saw lying on the ground. With the blade turned in, I held the blade's hilt in my hand, ready to slash if needed.

Zayne yelling, "I got your six!" offered some relief as I crouched, slashing upward at the scout in front of me, cutting up his chest. He grabbed at the flesh, blood now covering him, and I kicked him hard in his stomach. He stumbled back, slipping on the edge, and went down the long set of stairs that led to the front of the pack house, falling limp at the bottom.

I looked to my left; Juno was now in wolf form, fighting three wolves alone. I lunged and tackled one to the ground, and Zayne shifted, his wolf ripping out the throat of the one I held. Maybe it was because he trained me, but we made an effective team. I felt the body go limp in my arms, and with a brief struggle, managed to get out from under him.

Suddenly, our pack had the upper hand. The remaining Silver scouts, realizing they were now outmatched, retreated down the stairs and into the shadows.

Juno shifted back, panting and bruised. He glared at me: "I told you to stay in my room!"

"You're welcome!" I shot back. Dropping the knife and turning to leave, his hand on my wrist stopped me in my tracks.

I turned to look at him, anger flooding my system, but the painful look in his eyes dimmed the urge I had felt to haul off and punch him.

"I'm sorry," he said, his eyes falling. "What I should've said was, thank you."

"Yeah, well. I couldn't just do nothing."

"You handled yourself well. Are you hurt?" he asked, looking me over.

"I'm fine, Dad," I teased.

He wasn't amused. "Alec?" Juno asked.

"Yeah, I got clean-up. You go," Alec replied, waving us off as he reached down to take the pulse of the scout at his feet.

"This one's still alive," he said.

"Good, get him to the infirmary. Maybe we can get some information out of him," Juno ordered before returning his attention to me. "Let's get you cleaned up and into bed."

"I can take her to her room," Zayne chimed in, but Juno turned and whispered something in his ear.

Zayne's smile faded, replaced by a look of guilt.

"Stop. It isn't his fault. I was the one who chose to come; he was doing his job. We were *both* doing our job. Whether you like it or not." I didn't know what Juno had said to him, but I could guess.

"Let's go. Tomorrow's training will be long, and we're running out of time to prepare everyone, " he said, putting his hand on my lower back and attempting to lead me into the house.

"Don't touch me," I said, shoving his hand away.

As we re-entered the house, we walked in silence. I couldn't help but steal glances at the man beside me, wondering what thoughts spun behind those guarded eyes. The conversation with Flynn burned in my thoughts, a dangerous secret I dared not share. Revealing it would likely end with me in chains.

"Ezra..." he started, his voice a low rumble.

"No," I snapped, the word sharper than intended. "Go find Nyx. Isn't that her name? Seems more your type."

His gaze hardened. "You're sleeping in my room tonight. If they return, I need you where I can see you." The possessiveness in his tone was a tightening coil around my heart, a stark reminder of the gilded cage he offered.

My blood ran cold at his words, a mix of fear and defiance surging through me.

"You think a locked room will stop them?" I spat, my voice trembling despite my efforts. "If they want me, they'll find me. Keeping me prisoner won't protect me, it'll just make me hate you more."

I saw a flicker of something in his eyes—a flash of hurt, maybe even regret—but the familiar steel quickly masked it. "It's not up for discussion," he said, his voice low and dangerous. "I'm not losing you, not after everything." He reached for me again, but I flinched away, my heart pounding in my chest.

"Don't," I whispered, tears stinging my eyes. "Just...don't."

"You can sleep in the bed," he said as he began checking the windows and closing the curtains tightly.

"Or you could sleep in the bed, and I could go to *my* room."

His gaze turned glacial. "Get. In. The bed," he commanded, each word a stone. "Or I'll put you there myself." The threat hung in the air, unspoken but undeniable.

Grabbing a pillow, he made a makeshift bed on the floor, turning on his side, his back facing me so that he could keep watch on the door.

I surrendered to the bed, staring up at the ceiling, which remained indifferent to the thoughts swirling within, a relentless storm of anxieties and regrets, each one a barrier against the sweet oblivion of sleep. Sometimes my mind was truly my own worst enemy. The weight of guilt pressing down—Bash, Zayne, Juno, the scouts—the list only continued to grow, and with it…my inner torment.

No matter what position I tried, I only became more restless. I slammed a pillow over my head, the muffled scream a desperate plea against the confines of my mind. Frustration coiling within me.

"You're meant to be sleeping," Juno spoke, startling me. I thought he was sleeping, but his voice sounded tired and scratchy. I must've been keeping him awake, too.

"I'm sorry, it's just that my mind won't shut off," I whispered.

There was a bustle of movement in the dark, and then Juno slid into the bed next to me, "Come here, little toy," he said, his voice a low, seductive whisper. I felt his arm snake around my waist, pulling me closer. His breath was warm against my neck, sending shivers down my spine. I wanted to fight against the action, against him, but despite the hurt he continued to inflict, sometimes…he just knew what I needed.

The room was silent except for the sound of us breathing. The warmth of his body and his scent were comforting, and as I listened to the steady drum of his heart beating in his chest, I closed my eyes, surrendering to the moment. Whatever happened next was beyond my control.

Juno's touch was tender and possessive, his fingers tracing patterns on my skin. His whispered words filled the darkness, a symphony of desire and longing. Time seemed to stretch and bend, wrapping us in its embrace. "Close your eyes, little one. It's time to sleep now, so calm and safe in my arms."

Even in the quiet, his touch conveyed a thousand unspoken emotions. Each caress contradicted his harsh words from earlier. His very being riven between denying and embracing the depth of what we shared. The silence between us wasn't empty; it was filled with the weight of everything he couldn't bring himself to say.

***

The night sky was a tapestry of sorrow, the stars weeping silently as I ran, every step landing with a thunderous boom. The arena stretched before me, an endless expanse of shadow and despair. My breath came in ragged gasps, each step a Herculean effort as the ground beneath me stretched and elongated, mocking my desperate attempts to reach him.

"Bash!" I cried, my voice a haunting echo that was swallowed up by the oppressive darkness. I could see him, a mere silhouette in the distance. My legs burned with the effort, but no matter how fiercely I willed myself to move forward, the distance between us only grew.

Bash's eyes met mine, a fleeting moment of connection amidst the chaos. His expression was one of sorrow and resignation, as if he knew the end was near. The blade flashed in the dim light, a cruel and final punctuation to our love story.

"NO!" My scream tore through the night, a raw and primal sound reverberating through the arena. I fell to my knees. The ground beneath me was a cold, unyielding expanse until the nightmare tightened its grip, and the shadows began closing in, suffocating me with their cold embrace.

My scream seemed to stretch into eternity, echoing through the oppressive darkness of the nightmare. The shadows closed tighter around me, and I felt myself sinking into the abyss of despair. My breath came in short, panicked gasps, my heart pounding like a war drum in my chest.

"Ezra?" the voice was distant and distorted.

"Bash?" I whispered. "BAAASH!!!" I yelled again, clawing my way out of the darkness. A faint light appeared above me, a soft and gentle glow that seemed to beckon me towards it. As I clawed through the darkness, the light grew stronger and warmer, and as I felt its soothing touch wash over me, I heard the voice again.

***

"Ezra, WAKE UP!"

My eyes fluttered open, the nightmare dissolving like mist in the warmth of the morning sun. Juno was staring at me; his eyes filled with torment. I was in his bed, tangled in the sheets, my body drenched in a cold sweat. My labored breath tore through me, between quiet sobs. My heart was still racing from the terror of the dream as reality set in.

The room was dimly lit by the early morning light filtering through the curtains. I sat up. My hands were still trembling as I clutched the fabric of my oversized t-shirt. The memory of Bash's lifeless body lingered, refusing to fade. I couldn't contain the wave of nausea crashing over me. I pushed Juno to the side and swung my legs over the side of the bed. As I stood, the world around me seemed to tilt slightly. One hand cradling my belly, I began sprinting for the bathroom.

I slammed the door shut and barely made it to the sink; my reflection in the mirror was a blur as I leaned over, the sickness taking over. I convulsed and retched, the discomfort in my belly pouring out. Tears pricked at the corners of my eyes. When, finally, I stopped retching, the nausea slowly ebbing away, I took a deep breath.

Flipping on the faucet, I splashed the water on my face and swished it around in my mouth before spitting it into the sink. I opened the medicine cabinet and found mouthwash; I took a swig, gargling it around in my mouth and spitting it out, too.

I would've killed for a toothbrush, but this wasn't my room, so mouthwash it is. I straightened up, wiping my mouth with the back of my hand, when I heard three knocks on the door.

"You okay?" Juno asked through it.

"I just need a minute," I said as the door opened, and Juno entered. Rolling my eyes, I laughed. "Why bother knocking if you're just going to walk in?"

"Are you sick?" he asked.

"No, I'm okay. It was just a nightmare."

"Good. Training starts in twenty minutes; get dressed, and I'll walk you there."

Before I could argue, he was already out of the bathroom, and I was staring at the doorway. *Get dressed?* It's not like this was my room. I didn't have any clothes here.

"Clothes are in the closet." He spoke loud enough for me to hear, and I wondered if he could read my thoughts. I opened the closet door, and sure enough, many of my clothes were hanging up there.

"Un-fucking-believable, this guy," I said under my breath.

"Fifteen minutes."

"Yeah, I got it," I said, pulling out a set of clothes and getting dressed quickly, but my pants seemed a little snug. Bloated. Great, just what I freaking needed right now. I pulled my hair into a ponytail and headed to the bedroom.

"You just gonna stand there?" I teased as I walked past Juno and out of the door, knowing full well he'd been waiting here for me. When he fell into step beside me, I decided this was as good a time as any to confront him.

"Juno? Why are my things in your room?"

"Precautionary measures," he answered.

"For?" I asked, raising my brow.

"For just in case you stayed over and needed a change of clothes, my little toy," he jested, a low chuckle rumbling in his chest.

"Stop it. Don't do that…not when you're with Nyx. Not when…I'm not your toy, Juno," I said sternly. After a pause, I began firing off more questions. "And how did you know where my pantyhose were?"

"That first night, I cleaned you up, and…"

"You changed me. Yeah, okay, that's not weird or anything." I laughed. "How did you know that I went to Silver Pack that night…"

He deflected, asking a question of his own, "What's with all the questions?"

"It's just strange, and I wouldn't have to ask so many damn questions if you'd just be honest with me. Your games are exhausting."

He gave me a side-eye. Well, clearly, our little game of ask and tell was over, because when we got to the training grounds, he proceeded ahead and up to the podium without so much as a backward glance.

"Good talk," I spoke to…well, myself.

Zayne looked tired and had a cut on his cheek that I hadn't noticed last night when he headed my way, smiling. Always smiling, this guy.

"Hey Ezzie, you ready?" he asked.

"As I'll ever be," I said, following him to Dalton's mat.

"Dalton," I greeted.

"My Luna." He smiled. "I was instructed that today we will be working on defensive maneuvers."

"Awesome!" said Kit as she strode over, kissing Zayne on the lips, his cheeks burning bright red.

"Whaaaat?! Really?!" I yelled excitedly.

"Ezzie, have you met my official boyfriend?!" she gushed.

"Ah, that's amazing, you guys!" We were jumping up and down and squealing like we had just scored front-row tickets to an 'Arankai' concert! Drawing everyone's attention to us, including Juno's, a ghost of a smile dancing on his face.

But jumping up and down after being so sick this morning made me feel dizzy and lightheaded again. I should've stopped by the dining hall to get some food, especially with a full day of training ahead of me.

As I stopped jumping, I brought a hand to my forehead and suddenly struggled to stay upright.

"Ezzie?" Kit's voice was strained as her eyes darted around us. "Zayne, something's not right."

Zayne's arms wrapped around me, steadying me.

"I'm just…a bit. Dizzy," I said, falling into Zayne's arms. Dalton and Zayne helped me sit, and I scrunched my eyes, trying to focus. I saw Juno rushing toward me before everything went black.

CHAPTER FIFTEEN

Now That? That Was a Bad Idea.

Juno's POV

I grabbed Zayne by his collar, lifting him from the ground. "What the fuck did you do?!"

"Get your hands off of me," he said, squaring his shoulders. The kid had some balls; I'll give him that much.

"Stop it! He didn't do anything. She just passed out," Kit said. "Help me."

"Move," I said, dropping him and pulling Ezra into my arms.

Her breath was calm, even as I cradled her to my chest. I moved through the halls quickly and kicked the door to the infirmary open. *Shit. What if she had suffered an internal injury last night, and I was too stupid to notice?*

"Hang on, little one," I whispered as I hurried through the labyrinth of hallways that made up the infirmary. The air was thick with the scent of antiseptic, and the low hum of the fluorescent lights made me feel uneasy. I hated hospitals. I spent a lot of time in them when I was younger.

Back then, the days all seemed to blur together in a haze of sterile, white walls and the incessant beeping of machines. Every sound was a reminder of the fragile thread tethering Mom to this world. Watching her fade was like witnessing a slow-motion tragedy; each day was just a new entry in a chapter book nobody would ever want to read.

Dad and I would spend most nights there, and I'd sit by her side, holding her hand, feeling the frailty of her bones beneath my fingers, the warmth slowly ebbing away. Her once vibrant eyes had dulled over time from the pain and exhaustion that accompanied each new treatment until there was barely a flicker of the love and strength that had once defined her.

She always loved books, so I would sit beside her, my voice often trembling with the weight of the moment, and read to her. The cancer was relentless, a cruel thief stealing my mom day by day. As I read, I could feel my mother's hand tighten around mine, a silent plea for strength resonating through our touch.

The days turned into weeks. I watched her world shrink to the confines of her bed, and mine to that godforsaken hospital room. Her breaths became shallower, each one a struggle.

Until the day the beeping stopped. I was holding her hand as the room became eerily silent. Her skin was cold against mine, and reality crashed over me when I realized she was gone.

The world outside continued to turn, unaffected by the loss, but for me, time stood still.

"I need help," I told the nurse as she approached, a figure so calm as she guided me to a sterile bed.

"Is that our Luna?" she asked. "What happened?"

"She just…collapsed." My voice was trembling. "Please, help her." The memory of my mom haunted me, and I was left thinking worst-case scenario.

The nurse's hands moved with practiced grace, checking vitals and administering care. Time passed slowly, each minute lasting an eternity. Finally, the nurse turned to me. "Her vitals are all stable. I'll need to take a blood sample. It could be something as basic as low blood sugar. We should have the results in about an hour."

"Thank you, ma'am."

"Of course, Alpha. And Beta Alec is with that other gentleman. The one from last night's attack. He's awake if you'd like to speak with him."

"Of course, yeah, thank you," I said, standing and giving Ezra's hand one final, hesitant squeeze. I followed the nurse down the hall and into a small room. Inside lay the scout. He was secured to the bed and looked worse for wear. Alec was standing at the edge of the bed, a scalpel in hand.

"Woah, now," I said, holding my hand out, palm up.

With a frustrated grunt, Alec placed the scalpel in my hand.

"Alec, can you guard the door?" I asked, setting the scalpel down on the silver tray. "Nobody comes in," I ordered. He reluctantly nodded and exited the room.

"Not feeling too chatty today, are we?" I asked, looking down at the man before me.

"I'm loyal, unlike those pups you sent our way." He laughed, coughing and spitting blood.

"Ah, I see," I said, pulling a chair to the edge of the bed and sitting down, my eyes piercing, but my demeanor calm.

"Well, let's have a chat, shall we?" I paused before continuing. "I'm Alpha Black, and you're about to find out that this will go one of two ways...

Option one is that you can choose to cooperate and tell me what I want to know. Personally, I find that option quite boring, so I'm hoping for option two. This way we get to evaluate my surgical skills until you tell me what I want to know."

He didn't say a word.

Leaning forward, my voice a low, commanding whisper, I added, "Either way, I will get the information I desire."

"Fuck you!" he spat at me.

"Tell me what Gabe's planning," I said, standing up and digging through the drawers. I picked up what looked like some heavy-duty forceps. I'm reasonably sure these are meant to break bones. "Ah, perfect," I exclaimed as I showed them to the man strapped to the bed.

He shifted and squirmed uneasily in the bed, but was secured in a four-point restraint. He wasn't going anywhere, and we both knew it.

"Gabe's plans," I repeated, and again, he said nothing. I smiled, my lips curling up with a hint of wicked glee. "Option two, it is."

"Interesting fact about the human body. When someone loses a finger…" I placed the forceps over his pinky finger, squeezing it shut forcefully until I heard the satisfying snap of the knuckle joint crunching. He let out a horrifying scream, and I continued, "The body and brain will adapt to that loss. The remaining fingers become more…dexterous to compensate for the missing one," I continued. "But what happens when you lose more than one finger?"

I reset the forceps over his next finger and applied pressure again, this time more slowly. I could hear the bones splintering, and he was writhing in agony. His cries of pain seemed to echo in the small room, which I found incredibly annoying.

I continued, another snapping sound and more splintering bones, followed by another sharp scream ringing out.

"Oh shit, did you hear that one?" I laughed. This time, I watched his skin pale. I smacked him hard. "Oh no, no. We aren't done yet. Still seven fingers to go."

"Please, no more," he pleaded.

"Oh, come on now, we've just begun! After we finish with the fingers, there's also the toes."

"Please, I don't know about any plans," he stammered, his voice betraying his fear.

My gaze hardened, and I leaned closer. "Don't play games with me. We know Gabe has something planned. You were sent here to gather information, weren't you? Spill it, or things will get much worse for you."

The scout's eyes flickered with a mix of defiance and desperation.

"No?" I pulled my knife from the sheath at my side, stabbing it into his thigh. He cried out, his voice raw and filled with a mix of shock and torment. I twisted the blade, and the sound escaping the scout turned into a desperate, pained scream that echoed with primal fear and unbearable suffering.

"Well then, where were we? Oh, yes, here we go." I reset the forceps again, this time over his pointer finger.

"I… I can't," he muttered, his voice barely audible. "He'll kill me if I talk."

"How fortunate it is, then, that he is not here. But even more unfortunate for you, that I am," I warned. I could tell he was on the verge of breaking down. What a weak little shit. He doesn't deserve to live if he breaks after one torture session. The disloyal little fuck. But then again, if the scum doesn't talk, I'll simply kill him anyway.

He took a deep breath before he spoke, "He only asked us to locate your Luna's sleeping quarters. I don't know what he's planning or when."

"How large is your pack?" I asked. But he spat at me, "That's all you'll get out of me."

I lifted my shirt, wiping the blood/spit mixture off my face. "Now that? That was a bad idea."

Anger getting the better of me, I picked up the scalpel and held the man's head down, stabbing it into his eye socket; he let out a loud, screeching howl that echoed through the halls of the infirmary.

"My patience wanes, mutt. I'll ask once more: how large is your pack?"

The scout's face contorted in anguish as he struggled against the weight of his own fear. His remaining eye, now wide and haunted, reflected his inner turmoil as he writhed in pain.

"One hundred and twelve! In the pack, there are one hundred and twelve. Please, don't kill me. I have a family!" he cried out.

"Mercy, in the eyes of the ruthless, is but a fool's errand. A fleeting kindness that invites further betrayal and suffering."

"Please, Alpha Black, spare me," he pleaded.

"I'd be doing your family a disservice if I allowed such a disloyal, weak mutt to live," I spat at him as I ran the scalpel across his neck. Blood rapidly rushed out, soaking the bed all around him. Finally, everything was silent except for the gurgling sounds of blood and his last desperate gasps for air.

I opened the door to the hospital room, and Alec quickly noted the amount of blood on me.

"Alpha?" he asked.

"Clean-up, room six."

"Did you get anything useful?" he asked.

"A number. One-twelve. Minus the four we took out last night and this one. One hundred and seven."

"We outnumber them," he said.

"So it would seem. Also, between us. If this pathetic fuck was telling the truth, this whole war lives and dies with our Luna."

"Interesting. What are you thinking?" Alec asked.

"Meet me in the office in ten minutes."

"And room six?"

"Room six will still be there after we speak," I said, but first, I need to get cleaned up.

My eyes narrowed as I went to my room to shower and clean up before returning to Ezra, the weight of this decision pressing heavily on my chest. It's been thirty-six minutes since I left her, and I felt anxious to return, but with this current information ebbing away in my subconscious, I knew I needed to talk with Alec.

He's been my second in command since I took over Storm Cross Pack; if anyone understood my brain, it was him. Once I was cleaned up, all traces of the blood now gone, I got dressed and made my way to the office.

Alec was already waiting inside.

My heart was now a tangled web of emotions, warring with my head. I began working through my inner dialogue. "I'm thinking," I said, my voice low and measured, "that Gabe's obsessed with Ezra. His desire is wildfire. He will consume everything in his path until he gets to her."

My mind was a labyrinth of schemes, churning with a newfound purpose. "I understand the depths of Gabe's ambition—his need for her stems from Thorin. Thorin will never release his hold on her, and if Gabe gets the princess, he will also gain control of the empire. She's nothing more to him than a power play."

"Ezra has always been the key to Thorin's downfall," Alec said, mimicking my thoughts.

"That man is a titan of industry, but he's wronged many, including me," I said. The path to vengeance was clear to me now, but the cost was steep. I wasn't sure if I could use her as a pawn in my game of retribution any longer.

"Juno, we might be able to end this without more bloodshed if we can use her to our advantage, but..." Alec paused, a shadow of pain pulling at his heart, "the cost...could be her life. What is your revenge worth to you?"

I remained silent while I processed Alec's words. The agonizing silence enveloped the room, lifting the hairs on my arms and sending a shiver down my spine. My heart was aching at the thought of deceiving Ezra further, and yet the fire of vengeance burned brighter than ever.

I've been lying to her since the beginning, and I knew I could weave a larger tapestry of lies, and each thread would draw me closer to my goal. When the time came, I could strike, leaving her father in ruins. She thinks I want to ruin Gabe, but I don't. My fight has never been with him. I only seek to destroy her father.

"Are we willing to gamble with her life?" he whispered, his voice barely audible. "Is bringing your promise to fruition worth the sacrifice of our Luna? Or will we be consumed by the very darkness we seek to vanquish?"

"We will need a contingency plan."

"Juno, do you love her?" His question was sincere, but it had me stumbling for words. Love—now that's a scarier concept than war. And yet, I couldn't deny that she has become so much more to me than a pawn in this.

"If things go awry, we must be ready to extract her swiftly, Alec. I can't lose her, not now, not ever. But if she's the key, it's the play I've been waiting for all these years. We destroy him, and we protect her. She will remain unharmed in this," I replied, my voice steady despite the storm raging within. I don't know if I was trying to convince Alec or myself. I knew this would harm her, not physically, but emotionally. That girl was already fighting so hard to keep it together.

And it would be my hands that do the most damage. I was going to break her.

I knew that, and I hated myself for it.

"Understood," he replied with a reassuring pat on the shoulder. "We'll need our best Gamma on standby, ready to move at a moment's notice."

CHAPTER SIXTEEN

Please, Say Something.

Juno's POV

I stepped cautiously back into the hospital room, the distant drumming of my heart pounding in my ears. The soft hum of the medical equipment filled the air, making my stomach turn. The sickness grounded me, a backdrop to the swirling thoughts running amok in my head.

When I saw Ezra, the girl who crashed into my life, a whirlwind of chaos, love, and agony, I couldn't help but grin. She was now wide awake and gazing around with a mixture of confusion and fragility.

"Junior?" she murmured, her voice a fragile whisper. "What are you doing here?"

I hesitated. Whenever I saw this girl, I wanted to run to her, but I kept the shields firmly in place, my exterior calm, and my feet firmly planted where I stood just inside the doorway.

"Just checking on our Luna. How are you feeling?" I replied, my tone a careful balance of concern and restraint.

She looked at me, and it was like a switch flipped. Her eyes—Goddess, those eyes—blue, cerulean depths like a clear sky, but they cut right through me. How could I not lose it? Every second with her was a battle, wanting to tear down every wall I had built, even though I knew I shouldn't. It was torture, pure and simple, and I was losing.

"But why?" she asked. "Does Nyx know where you are?"

Before I could respond, the nurse from earlier entered. She glanced at the chart in her hands and then looked up at both of us as if she sensed the unspoken tension that lingered there. "Oh, good, she's awake. Luna?" the nurse began. "Due to the nature of your visit with us today, we ran some bloodwork."

"And?" Ezra questioned.

"And, well, the labs have returned. It appears that you, our sweet Luna, are carrying a pup. It's still too early to know precisely how far along you are, but based on these levels, I'd guess between three to six weeks."

The nurse's words hung in the air, a revelation that shifted the very fabric of our reality. Ezra was *pregnant*.

Ezra's eyes widened, her confusion deepening. My face remained blank, but inside I was a mess of feelings— happiness? Maybe that was there, but also a ton of *what now?* This wasn't how it was supposed to go. We were supposed to have more time to figure things out. Now, it was all different, and I had no clue what to do next.

Ezra's POV

I was frozen. I could barely process the words.

The weight of my past, the scars of that abuse, and the haunting memory of my mother's abandonment all crashed over me at once—a wave of fear, confusion, then a flicker of hope.

My hand brushed over the lowest part of my stomach. My heart was racing faster than I'm sure was humanly possible, like the wistful wingbeats of a gentle hummingbird.

My body's response to those words was sudden and unforgiving, a creeping sensation as the flutter in my chest escalated. Each thud echoed in the silence of the room. My breath was shallow, and the air around me was thick, making it impossible to draw a full breath.

Could it be?

My chest tightened, a sense of impending doom washing over me, and an inexplicable fear gripping at the entirety of my being. My hand against my belly, now trembling, felt cold and shaky against my skin, grounding yet unsettling as the raw emotion coursed through my veins.

The edges of the room dissolved around me, just like the darkness in my nightmares had for the last few weeks. Each shadow was a phantom reaching out, pulling me into its clutches. Unrelenting as the walls tunneled around me, blurring the lines between reality and nightmare, becoming indistinguishable. All I could focus on was the nausea now churning in my belly.

Oh Goddess.

Was this Bash's child? Was I carrying the last piece of him? My most authentic love, the one who had been taken from me far too soon? Is that what the nightmares were trying to tell me?

Or was it his? I looked up at Juno…the one who confused my heart with his hot and cold demeanor. Yet, despite all the confusion and chaos born into this world when we were together, I couldn't help but think maybe that wouldn't be the worst thing…because when I thought of Bash, all it brought with it was pain.

How was I supposed to hold the child of my dead mate and not be reminded daily of all that he was to me or that I had killed him? It was my fault. How would I ever explain that to our child?

I looked up at Juno, needing some reassurance. His presence suddenly became a beacon, guiding me to him and drawing me in. Knowing that he was here with me brought me some comfort, although he was never mine.

"What if…this baby is his?" I whispered, my voice barely audible. "Juno…what if it's yours?"

He stepped closer, his brows furrowed, pained. He sat on the edge of the bed, pulling me into his chest, and I felt the storm beginning to pass. My heart beats, slowing in the calmness of his embrace. The tightness in my chest began to ease, and my breaths began to steady.

Yet, a lingering unease remained—a shadow of panic. Tears welled up in my eyes and fell in thick lines down my face.

Say something. *Please, say something.* I pleaded without uttering a word as I leaned into his embrace, still sniffling.

"Calm yourself, little one. You are so much stronger than you know." His words brushed over my cheeks; his warm breath was cool against the wet trails where tears had fallen.

"It doesn't matter what the answer is; this child is a part of you, making it precious to me."

"Even though you hate me?"

"Oh, you stupid girl." He laughed, pulling me closer to him. "I could never hate you. If anything, I think I care a little too deeply about you."

"But…Nyx."

"Shhh, Nyx never *was* or *will* be anything more than a friend."

My voice dripped with sarcasm and hurt as I sniffled and wiped my tears on the sleeve of my hospital gown. "What? But you said it was a mistake," I murmured.

"I lied," Juno whispered, his eyes downcast, shadows of regret flickering across his face.

"I know, I felt it." I laughed, a hollow sound that echoed in the tense silence. "What are we going to do?"

"I don't know. But whatever it is, we will face it together," Juno replied, his voice resolute, determination hardening his features.

"Gabe…" I began, the name hanging heavily in the air as the nurse returned.

"What about him, Ezra? Oh shit, don't you dare tell me that he could be the father, too." A new fire ignited in his eyes, the flames of anger and protectiveness mingling behind the dark black irises that were fixed on me.

"I'm so sorry, Alpha. Luna. I just wanted to bring in your discharge instructions; I also took it upon myself to prescribe a prenatal vitamin," the nurse said, handing me a stack of papers.

"Thank you," I whispered, taking the papers and offering her an apologetic smile before I turned back to Junior. I hadn't realized she was still standing there, and truthfully…it had startled me when she spoke. This was an incredibly private conversation, and so I hesitated, the weight of the truth pressing down on me.

Once the nurse excused herself, I stood up from the bed. "No," I said firmly, shaking my head. "He can't be. I made sure of it."

Juno's eyes widened, relief washing over his features. "You did?"

"Yes," I confirmed, my voice steady. "I took Plan B right after. There's no way he could be the father."

Juno sighed, the tension easing from his shoulders. "Okay," he muttered, pulling me into a tight embrace. "I don't know what I would've done if…"

"We don't have to think about that," I interrupted gently, resting my head against his chest.

Juno nodded, his grip tightening around me. "You're right. So, what about him then?"

The resolve in his voice was like a balm to my frayed nerves. I allowed myself to hope for the first time in what felt like ages. But I also knew I needed to tell him about my conversation with Flynn.

"Well, I called Flynn."

"Flynn? I thought we were talking about Gabe."

"We ARE talking about Gabe. Flynn was Kit's and my roommate in college before, well, all this bullshit started, but she's a part of the Silver Pack. Just, will you let me fucking talk?"

He chuckled again, ushering his hands before him as he gave me the floor. It was obnoxious how much his cocky little smile drove me crazy, and I rolled my eyes before sighing heavily and laughing.

"Anyways, I called her, and…"

"When was this?" he asked.

"I don't know, before that attack yesterday, why?" I was annoyed that he, yet again, interrupted me. But also, why the fuck does it matter when I called her?

"You called someone from our rival pack and didn't think to share this information with me until now?" He pulled away from me.

He was angry again, and I was back to exceedingly confused. Sometimes, I couldn't tell if Junior was with me or against me.

"You told me to stay the fuck out of your way, remember?"

I didn't understand what I did so wrong. He didn't want to give me any fucking information, forcing me to go down a different avenue to find it on my own.

But Junior's eyes were unmistakable. They blazed with frustration, his breath coming in sharp bursts. "Staying out of my way doesn't mean keeping secrets and putting yourself yet again at risk," he growled, his voice a low rumble that sent shivers down my spine.

I clenched my fists, trying to steady my racing heart. "Secrets? It was just a call. I didn't think it was important."

"Not important?" He took a step closer, his presence overwhelming. "Every move we make matters, especially now."

I met his gaze, defiance burning in my eyes. "I know that! And what about you? You keep me in the dark half the time. How am I supposed to know what is or isn't important?"

His expression softened momentarily before the mask of anger returned. "We're in this together, whether you like it or not. Next time, you tell me everything."

"Usually, that's my line." I laughed, but he didn't. He shook his head in disbelief as he palmed his forehead and rubbed his temples.

"Great. Are we done fighting now? I want to tell you what Flynn said," I asked, standing up and grabbing his hand. He nodded, the tension between us crackling like a storm about to break.

"Fine." He sighed, the fight draining out of him.

"I'm fairly certain that Gabe plans to attack along the border to draw the fight away from the main pack house sometime within the next four weeks."

"Fairly certain? Why would he attack indirectly when he believes he can overpower us?" he asked.

"I'm pretty sure there is only one target."

"How do we know we can trust this Flynn person? This could be misinformation. If we prepare for this, and we're wrong, we'd be caught completely off guard." He was pacing the room now.

After a brief time, he returned to me, cradling me in his arms. He was quiet, not uttering a word as he breathed me in. When he did speak, I felt the pain his voice portrayed. "He wants to draw the fight away from you."

"This was always about me," I said, confirming his suspicion, wrapping my arms around his neck.

"He will never have you."

"I know, but…"

"He will *NEVER* have you! You are MINE."

I swear, sometimes, the stubbornness of this man.

I pinched his face, pulling his gaze to mine, "First-off, I'm sick of everyone thinking, I am an object that can be possessed. Second, please listen to me. We can destroy him. Just let me talk with—"

"Ezra," he warned, cocking his head to the side and pulling away.

"If I can just get him to—"

"No."

"Will you not just hear me out?" I whined.

"When will you see? I cannot have you in harm's way. I will always choose to protect you—and the baby. I'll find another way," he said, getting up and leaving the room.

When he walked away, I couldn't shake the feeling that this was far from over. The lines between us had blurred, leaving me wondering where we truly stood.

CHAPTER SEVENTEEN

Prophetic Child

Ezra's POV

My mind was, well, a mess. The night was cloaked in velvet darkness, the stars shimmering like scattered diamonds across the sky. I sat by the window, my hand resting gently on my abdomen, a whirlwind of emotions swirling through my mind.

The open window let the cold breeze in. It came in sharp bursts, whirling around me, and was soothing against the heat radiating from my skin. The realization hit me like a ten-ton Mack truck: I was *pregnant.*

If you'd asked me last year what my expectations were for my future, I guarantee that Luna of not one, but two wolf packs would never have been included in that list. Outliving the death of my fated mate—also not on that list. Pregnant, unsure of the father, and barely eighteen—yet another challenge I had never expected to face.

"How did we get here?" I asked, looking up at the glowing moon above. I suppose I was speaking to the Moon Goddess. I had always prayed to her, and though she never replied, I felt her presence, as if she were always there, silently listening.

This world had always been shrouded in darkness, and I had endured endless suffering. Yet, praying to our most sacred being helped me, and I often spoke to her. Each silent prayer became a whisper carried away on the winds, a connection to something greater.

I poured my thoughts and fears into those sacred moments, seeking comfort in the silence that followed. If anyone could understand the unspoken pain and offer a sense of peace in the chaos of life, it was her.

My thoughts tonight were a tangled web of confusion and fear. How was I supposed to raise a child? How was I supposed to be a mother when I had never had one to show me what to do? Did I even want to be a mother? What if I failed at it…

A soft knock on the door pulled me away from my reverie. Kit entered my room, a concerned look on her face. I hadn't told her or anyone else about the baby yet.

"Ezra, what's wrong? You've been so quiet tonight. We were all so scared, and it seems like you've been avoiding us," she said, pushing a stray lock of hair behind her ear.

"Us?"

"Hey!" Zayne greeted me from behind her, and a soft giggle escaped me.

"I'm glad you're both here," I said, turning back to the window.

"So, do you want to talk about it? Or we can sneak into the kitchen and make some massive sundaes, all the works!" Zayne said, falling with a thump on my bed.

"Zayne, I told you she doesn't like ice cream," Kit scolded him.

"Well, I was hoping you were wrong. Ice cream sounds awesome right now."

"She's right; I don't like ice cream." I laughed. "And ugh, let's not talk about it. I might be sick again, just thinking about the stuff. So cold and sugary. Just yuck!"

"You're an absolute freak of nature," he teased, throwing a pillow at me; I caught it but exclaimed, "Hey now, what did the baby ever do to you?"

Suddenly, both of their gazes landed on my hand that lay over my abdomen.

Kit's eyes widened, a mix of shock and concern in them. "Pregnant? Ezzie, how…I mean, do you know who the father is?"

I shook my head. The truth is, I had no idea. "I don't know, Kit. It could be Juno's or Bash's. And…I don't even know what to hope for."

Kit's face hardened at the mention of Juno. "Ezra, you know how I feel about Juno. He's dangerous, and I can't bear the thought of you being tied to him through a child. Bash, on the other hand…he was so good for you."

I felt my heart twisting. I loved Bash with all my heart, but he was gone. And there was something about Juno that kept drawing me in, a dark magnetism…that I couldn't explain.

"I know, Kit. But I can't deny that part of me is drawn to him. It's like he's a part of me, and I don't understand it any more than you do."

"What are you going to do?" Zayne asked.

It was a fair question. I had options to consider. I mean, how is an eighteen-year-old girl supposed to raise a child? I didn't have to ask Zayne; I knew he would also be praying this child was Bash's. The baby would be a part of him that we could both hold onto, despite his absence from our lives. But if the child wasn't his, did I want to keep it? How could I raise a child amidst a war? Alongside a man like Junior Black?

"I don't know, Zayne. If this baby is Bash's…what does that mean for our alliance? And…if it's Juno's, what does that mean for me? For us? Is he even capable…of being a father? I barely know him."

"Ezra, I've told you before," he paused, "and I'll never stop saying it because I will always mean it. No matter what, we will stand with you. Kit and I will support

you through this, but you must decide what *you* want.
What is your heart telling you?"

I closed my eyes, trying to listen to the whispers of
my heart. I felt the pull of both men, the light and the
dark. I wasn't sure if I could be a mother, but I knew that I
wanted to fight for my child, just as someone should have
fought for me.

"I just want what's best for the baby," I said finally. "I
want them to grow up safe and loved. But how do we even
do that when we're at war?"

"Together." He smiled.

"He's right, even if he is a big ol' knucklehead. We
will figure it out together, just as we always do. We will
protect our pack prince or princess," Kit exclaimed.

"Hey, I'm gonna make you pay for that little
comment later," Zayne said, pulling Kit down into his lap
and tickling her. Her giggles filled the room, and
everything was light.

A glimmer of hope amidst the turmoil. I knew the
road ahead would be challenging, but with Kit and Zayne
at my side, I always felt a little stronger, a little braver.

"You two really want me to lose my dinner, don't
you?" I said, heavy on the sarcasm. "Why don't you two go
enjoy some of that icky sugar from the kitchen?" I laughed.
"I should probably try to get some rest, anyway. It's been a
long ass day."

"Yesssss!" Zayne yelled, jumping up from the bed. He hugged me and said, "I'll wait outside. Don't keep my girl too long, though, Ezra. We have plans."

"Again, ew," I groaned, and then I hugged Kit tight. "You two are so cute, it's gross."

"I know. It's great. I honestly don't know how I got so lucky," she gushed.

"Get out of here, have fun, and I'll see you tomorrow. I love you."

"Love you, too, babes! And…if you need me, just call. Okay?"

Once they were gone, I was once again alone with my thoughts. I tossed and turned in bed uncomfortably before peeking at the alarm clock. 1:15 in the morning.

Well, that's just great.

The night was silent, except for the croaking of the Katydids. The world slumbered under a blanket of stars, and I started counting the croaks. The nightmares had come every night for the last few weeks, and I found myself fighting more and more against their dark embrace.

One. Two. Threeee…Four…

***

As the night around me drifted away, I was drawn into a dreamscape of ethereal beauty. Unlike my previous nightmares, this one wasn't encased in darkness. I was standing in a vast, moonlit meadow, the silvery light casting an otherworldly glow on the flowers at my feet, which swayed gently in a phantom breeze.

The essence of each bloom filled my nose, a symphony of earthy and spicy scents. A soft chuckle escaped me as I moved forward, my fingers dancing across the vibrant hues and delicate textures. Closing my eyes, I inhaled the sheer beauty that surrounded me, a world suspended in time. The atmosphere was hushed, serene, as if holding its breath, and a memory began to bloom—the greenhouse, our sanctuary.

But as my eyes fluttered open, I realized this was no mere memory. It was real, vivid, breathing before me—perhaps a dream, or a trick of the heart, but undeniably there. I didn't hesitate, not even for a heartbeat, before sprinting forward. I was afraid it would vanish, forever just out of reach, like he'd been every night prior. Yet, it remained.

Bursting through the door, my breath hitched, tears stinging my eyes with a bittersweet familiarity. "Bash?" My voice trembled, a fragile whisper in the stillness.

His smile, a radiant sunrise, warmed me to my core. His eyes were endless pools reflecting a love that transcended worlds, holding me captive. "I swore on the Goddess that I would hold you again, my love. The silver moon, our eternal witness, remembers my vow."

"You're here? This…it's really you?" My voice cracked, disbelief warring with a desperate hope. "But how? How is this possible?"

He enfolded me in his arms, and warmth bloomed in my belly, chasing away the lingering chill of sorrow. I melted into his embrace, allowing myself to believe, if only for a moment, that he was truly there, whole and mine once more.

"It's been so hard without you," I cried.

His fingers wiped away the tears, forcing my gaze to his. "Ezzie, please, you know I hate it when you cry."

Clinging to him, I buried my face in his chest, inhaling the scent of pine and earth that clung to his clothes, a scent I thought I'd lost forever. "I miss you," I choked out, the words raw and ragged. "Every second of every day. It hurts, Bash. It still hurts so much."

He held me tighter, his fingers tracing light circles against my skin, a familiar comfort that sent shivers down my spine. "I know, baby girl," he murmured. "I know it does. But you are strong, my love. Stronger than you realize."

Pulling back slightly, I looked up at him, my eyes searching his. "But why? Why did you have to leave? We were supposed to have forever."

A shadow crossed his face, a fleeting glimpse of the pain he carried. "Forever is not always measured in time, Ezzie," he said softly. "Sometimes, it's measured in moments. And the moments we shared? They are etched into eternity."

He cupped my face in his hands, his thumbs gently wiping away the tears that streamed down my cheeks. "Don't mourn my absence. Celebrate our love. Carry it with you, let it guide you, let it give you strength. And know that I am always with you, in the whisper of the wind, in the warmth of the sun, in the love that beats within your heart."

His words were like a melody, a bittersweet song that both soothed and broke my heart. "But it's not the same," I whispered, my voice trembling. "It will never be the same."

"No," he admitted, his eyes filled with profound sadness. "It won't. But that doesn't mean it can't be beautiful. You have a new life to live, Ezzie—a purpose to fulfill. Don't let my death be your ending. Let it be your beginning. For you and Ayanna."

The unfamiliar name hung in the air between us, a fragile, unspoken promise. "Ayanna?" I questioned, the word catching in my throat like a sob.

His hand, warm and familiar, moved to rest gently on my abdomen, a silent caress that sent a jolt of electricity through my veins. I looked up at him, my brow furrowed in confusion, my heart pounding in my chest like a trapped bird. "It means 'beautiful flower'," he whispered, his gaze tender and knowing.

A wave of dizziness washed over me, the world tilting on its axis. "You know?" I breathed, my voice barely audible, my mind struggling to grasp the weight of his words, when suddenly, a blinding light illuminated the darkness. Instinctively, I pivoted, my hand outstretched in a futile attempt to shield my eyes from its ethereal glow.

From it, the most radiant figure descended, materializing before me and stealing my breath. "Child of fire and fate," the iridescent figure spoke, her voice like a soft rustle of leaves in the wind. "You carry within you a spark of destiny."

"Child of fire and fate? I don't understand. What do you know of me?" I whispered, bewildered.

"I know you well, child of the moon, for I am Selene."

"You're the…Moon Goddess?"

"I am."

Before I could wrap my mind around standing face to face with Selene, Bash's voice pulled me back to him. "Ezzie?" he spoke, but his essence was slowly ebbing away like moonlight on a dissipating mist. Turning towards him, I fell to my knees, begging. "Please, don't leave me again!" I cried, my voice a barely audible sound. "Please?! Bash?! I need you…"

He pulled me back to him, cradling me in his arms before leaning into me. His lips meeting mine with an intensity that spoke volumes, a dance of passion and tenderness beautifully intertwined. The kiss deepened, a silent promise of longing and unspoken words. It was the type of kiss that lingered in the soul, a touch that would be remembered long after our parting, a goodbye that was anything but final.

"Baby girl, remember the good times we had, the quiet moments, the dreams we shared. Keep them close, but do not let them consume you. Keep Ayanna safe. And know that I will always love you."

"Is the little one..." My voice cracked as he shimmered, dissolving before my very eyes, his form becoming less defined with each passing moment.

The unspoken question hung in the air, a plea for reassurance and a desperate attempt to hold onto the last vestiges of our love. With tears streaming down my face, I reached out to touch him, my fingers grasping at the fading light where his form used to be.

His eyes, filled with a mixture of love and sorrow, met mine, conveying a message of hope and resilience. Though his physical form was disappearing, his spirit would forever remain intertwined with mine, a celestial bond that transcended the boundaries of life and death.

"GIVE HIM BACK TO ME!" I yelled at the Goddess. "PLEASE!? Please, I'm begging you! Give him back to me..."

The Moon Goddess extended a hand, and the meadow transformed. Before my eyes, a vision unfolded—a beautiful red-haired child, my child, standing at the edge of a great forest, bathed in moonlight.

The child turned, and her eyes shone with a fierce, gentle light, a beacon of hope and strength.

"This child," the goddess continued, "is destined to bridge the realms of light and shadow. They will possess the power to heal the ever-growing rift that divides our world, to bring balance where there is chaos. Her potential will be limitless, but

so will her trials be, meant to assess her spirit and resolve; do not let the child walk alone."

The vision shifted, and Juno and I stood together, our hands intertwined. The little one danced around us…shimmering, unbreakable bonds connecting the three of us.

"Juno?"

"You must prepare the child, guide them with love and wisdom. The path ahead will be fraught with danger, but together, you will forge a harmonious future where light and dark coexist."

"But why does it have to be this way? Goddess, I don't understand. Why my child?"

"The Child of Your Blood. The Prophetic Child will face the 'Temptation of Darkness' where the shadows whisper promises of power and dominion, seeking to sway her heart. The allure of the shadow realm will be strong, and they must summon the strength to resist, to remain true to their mission."

The meadow shifted. I looked at my child standing on a precipice, the sun's blinding light casting harsh shadows.

"The Blinding Light will also test them," the Goddess continued. "In their pursuit of purity and righteousness, they may be tempted to forsake the shadows, to become unyielding and uncompromising. They must learn that true balance requires embracing both light and dark."

As the dream faded, the Moon Goddess touched my shoulder gently.

"Remember, the light of the moon will always watch over you. You are a child of Fire and Fate. Trust in Lana, she will guide you. Trust in your strength, and in the strength of those who stand with you."

***

I awoke startled, the echoes of the dream lingering in my mind. *"A dream?"* I questioned, but it felt so real…

Perhaps it was the gnawing ache of his absence that fueled it, an attempt by my subconscious to relive the moments Bash and I had shared. Yet, as the reality of his departure crashed down upon me, a renewed sense of determination began to bloom amidst the pain. Like a solitary flower pushing through the cracks in the pavement, I resolved to carry his memory with me, using it as a beacon to guide me and Ayanna through the darkness.

Though the dream had ended too soon, leaving me yearning for more, I knew that Bash's spirit would forever remain a part of me. And with that realization, I rose from my bed, ready to face whatever challenges lay ahead, knowing that I was not alone, for his love would always be my strength.

For this child.

My child.

The child of my blood.

CHAPTER EIGHTEEN

Show Them What You're Made Of

Ezra's POV

"I am not broken. Just because I'm pregnant does not mean—"

"Luna, that is the heir to our pack," Dalton cut me off. It's been like this ever since the news of my pregnancy had cycled through the rumor mill, and I was finding it hard to suppress the anger coursing in my veins. I was no different today than I was last week.

"You will sit this one out," Dalton ordered, putting his arm out to stop me.

"Like HELL I WILL!" I said, pushing past him.

It seemed like all the work I had put into my training—the small win I had felt when the pack accepted me—was all for nothing. The idea of anyone telling me what I could or couldn't do wasn't one I was willing to accept anymore. I was stronger now, different. I was Luna of this goddamn pack. If anyone was going to protect my child, it was me.

I stepped up onto the mat. Immediately, the wolf before me tapped out, stepping down from the mat.

"Are you kidding me?" I asked as I stabbed my sword into the mat and began pacing.

"Will no one help their Luna train?" I asked, and even Zayne's eyes turned down. He was sure this was Bash's heir. He would never risk the baby's fragile little life, and I didn't blame him for his decision. It was his to make. I couldn't blame anyone for their concern, but I might as well be living in a padded room with the level of caution everyone was taking with this tiny pup's life.

"Pick up your sword." I turned to see Beth before me. I hadn't seen or heard from her much since the war had begun. It took me a minute to register her words. I pulled my sword from the ground and readied myself.

"Beth?!" Zayne yelled. "Stand down. What do you think you're doing?"

"What good is a Luna who cannot defend herself or her pack?" Beth shot back at her brother before swinging her sword down swiftly; I blocked and pushed her back.

"None of you jackasses are doing her any favors!" she yelled, striking again. I stepped to the side and swung my sword up, which she blocked.

Beth's eyes glinted with fierce determination as she pressed forward, her movements swift and precise.

I was in awe of her strength and skill. Regardless of being such a princess, it was clear she had been training her whole life. She was meant to be the Luna; that was the position her father had planned for her in our pack. She would have been an excellent Luna, but Bash had chosen me.

I thought about last year, how despite her shitty disposition toward me most days, she had shown up when I needed that extra push. And now, when everyone else refused to see the me that existed beyond this pregnancy, she again stepped up. A whole new appreciation was budding in my heart for this girl.

"This is what she needs!" she shouted, her voice echoing through the training grounds. "Strength, not coddling!"

I felt the adrenaline surge through me, matching her intensity. Our swords clashed repeatedly, the metallic ring resonating with each strike. "I won't break," I growled, meeting her gaze fiercely. "I will protect my pack, no matter what."

Beth smirked, a fierce pride in her eyes. "That's the Luna I know," she said, stepping back slightly, giving me room to advance.

Juno approached the mat. He didn't speak; he folded his hands over his chest and watched.

"Show them what you're made of," Beth whispered.

With a renewed sense of vigor, I lunged forward, our swords dancing in a deadly ballet. The pack watched in stunned silence, the air thick with tension. Each move, each parry, was a testament to my resolve.

As our blades locked, Beth leaned in, her voice low but firm. "Prove them wrong, Luna. Show them how strong you are. Show them your heart."

I nodded, determination blazing in my eyes. This was my fight, my moment. And I would not back down.

With a final, mighty shove that encapsulated the determination within, I pushed Beth back, our swords separating with a sharp clang. She stumbled slightly, but her eyes were filled with pride. "That's it, Luna," she said, breathing heavily.

I turned to face the pack, my chest heaving with exertion. "I am not fragile," I declared, my voice strong and unwavering. "I am not broken. And I will fight for this pack, my family, and our future."

The silence was deafening. Then, one by one, heads began to nod. Zayne stepped forward; his eyes filled with respect. "Alright, Luna," he said quietly. "We'll train together."

I nodded, feeling a weight lift off my shoulders. I stood proud amongst my brothers and sisters.

Beth grinned, sheathing her sword. "Now that that's settled, let's get to work."

And with that, the tension began to dissipate. The pack members stepped forward, ready to train, ready to fight. And I knew, in that moment, it wasn't my pack's acceptance I needed. It was mine. I was so much more than the girl I had been. My past did not define me.

Juno stepped up on the mat, suddenly turning me. He grabbed my sword, yanking it out of my hand in one swift motion before tossing it to Zayne. Then he pulled me into a firm embrace, his voice a low growl in my ear. "Why do you insist on putting yourself in danger?"

Juno's grip on me was firm, almost desperate, as he held me in his arms. I could feel the tension in his muscles as they pressed into my tiny frame. His breath was hot against my ear; each word laced with trepidation when he spoke again.

"Do you have any idea what it feels like? Watching you risk everything?" His voice cracked.

I pulled back slightly, just enough to look into his eyes. They were stormy, a tumult of worry and love that took my breath away. I knew he hated it when I put myself in danger. This wasn't like that. I needed to prove to myself that I could do it.

"Juno, I had to. They needed to see me in this way. They needed to know that no matter the risk, I would fight for them!"

His head shook, his hands gripping my shoulders in a desperate attempt to be heard. "No matter the risk? Your life is a cost I will never be willing to pay. Not now. Not ever."

"Because you love me?" I teased.

"Because I profoundly care about you."

The weight of his words resonated like an echo between us. If I thought he had any, I would've sworn that was genuine fear in his eyes. I placed a hand on his cheek, my voice soft. "I promise to be careful, my Alpha. But I cannot stop fighting. Not now. And I think I 'profoundly care about you,' too."

Junior sighed, his anger melting away into a weary acceptance. He pressed his lips firmly to mine. The kiss was possessive and fierce, like a tempest gathering in the recesses of his being. Almost primal.

"Stop. Juno, what are you doing?" I asked him quietly as I pulled away from the kiss, well aware that all of our warriors were still gathered around us.

"I want you, " he said with a self-assured charm and confident smirk, and I knew that he meant, *If I want you, then I will have you.*

"Not the time or the place," I scolded him.

"Training is over," he shouted over my shoulder as he lifted me from the mat and carried me out of the grounds.

My brows furrowed. I'm sure it probably looked ridiculous; their Alpha was carrying me out of training. But I didn't care. It had been too long since I had felt him. I'll admit it, every ounce of my body was crying out for him.

We entered the pack house, and he immediately walked into the first door on the left. And I couldn't help but laugh, "Juno, this is the library. We are not having sex here!!"

Without a word, he set me down on the long sofa, his hand reaching up to my ponytail. Gently, he tugged at it, a mischievous glint in his eyes. "The bedroom is too far away," he murmured, my hair falling in a messy tangle along the sides of my face as he pulled the band out. I pushed against his chest, trying unsuccessfully to put some distance between our bodies.

He can't really be serious. We cannot have sex in the middle of the pack library. Had he lost his mind?

But his knee slid between my thighs; his hand moved in soft strokes along the side of my face with an unexpected tenderness that made my breath hitch as he coerced me into lying down. He positioned his body over mine. My hands fell in defeat, resting against his chest.

I began fidgeting, tracing circles against the exposed hair on his chest while my heart kicked into overdrive. I looked up at him, confused by his lack of force and even more by my body's willingness to succumb without the commanding demeanor I had grown used to.

Another strange shift in what we had been.

"Juno, I don't..." My pleas were cut short by his thumb tracing over my bottom lip. Pulling down on it, his lips gently captured mine, sucking my plump bottom lip into his mouth. I felt his canines biting down. The sharp pain brought with it a sense of pleasure as his tongue began swirling with mine. The faintness of blood filled both our mouths, but there was something so intimate about it.

His other hand was moving down my body. He squeezed the soft, fleshy area on the side of my waist, pushing my hips down before pulling me closer to him. The movement fueled the burning desire to feel him, have him, and be enveloped in his warmth—a yearning that danced like flames in my heart, a longing that whispered with every heartbeat.

When his phone began ringing, he released my side and pulled it from his jeans. His mouth pulled away just enough so that he could see to hit *end call* before dropping his phone to the floor beside us and deepening the kiss again.

He dipped his finger into the hem of my leggings, making me breathe heavily as his finger trailed down my side before gripping my ass. His other hand braced his weight as he began rolling his hips against me, and I'm telling you this man could have easily joined the cast of *Magic Mike*.

With his perfectly toned physique, well-sculpted muscles, and the way his dick was rubbing against me, I was sure that if he'd go down on me right now, he'd have drowned. A needy moan escaped my lips as a smile played against his.

"Dolly," he breathed, "I lo—"

The sudden, insistent ringing of Juno's phone again shattered the bubble of our private moment, and a frustrated sigh escaped him. I ran my hands through his hair and cupped the back of his neck in my hands.

"It's okay, answer it," I said.

Reluctantly, he sat up, and I moved into a sitting position beside him, pulling my knees to my chest. He reached down, found the phone, put it on speakerphone, and set it on the coffee table.

"Alec? This better be important," he grumbled.

Alec's voice was urgent. "Alpha, Elder Thorin is outside. He's alone, but he's demanding to see Ezra."

My heart plummeted as Alec spoke, and I gripped my knees tighter to my chest as my body shrank into the sofa. The name alone sent a chill down my spine. Memories of my father, the harsh words, the stinging blows, surged forward. The tranquility of the moments just shared with Juno was shattered as I felt the familiar grip of fear tightening around my heart.

"Keep him outside, Alec. Don't let him in," Juno ordered before ending the call. I vaguely remember him pulling me into his side, my face nuzzling into his chest as he clung to me, and my body trembled beneath his touch. It was instinctive, like that was where I belonged, safely tucked into his side.

"Why now?" I whispered, my voice almost breaking.

Juno wrapped his arms tighter around me, trying to offer some relative comfort as I struggled to make sense of the chaos in my mind. My hands fisted, and I could feel my nails digging into my palms in an attempt to ground myself.

Fear was no stranger to me. It had once dictated my every move. Hearing my dad's name brought back those whispered warnings: *"Remember the pain, the betrayal. It's safer to stay guarded, to keep your distance. You have no power. He will destroy you."*

But anger, or rather Lana, roared back.

"Why should he have this power over you still? You're stronger now. Don't let his shadow control your life anymore."

She was right. I should've cried my last tear for that man nearly a year ago. I straightened up, wiping my arm against my face—the last drops bearing witness to the fury that now simmered just below the surface.

"You have nothing to be afraid of, dolly. He can't hurt you. I won't let him. I will protect you and our family." His hand fell on my lower stomach, and I knew it didn't matter whose baby this was. Junior was prepared to give this child all of his love.

A choked laugh escaped my lips, "I'm not afraid," I mused, looking up at him. "I'm pissed, Juno."

Fear may have held sway when I was isolated and alone, but now, I was surrounded by my chosen family: my friends, my wolf, Bash's eternal love, Ayanna, and *Juno.* This was no longer a mere alliance; we had forged something beautiful amidst the darkness, regardless of how our situation had been thrust upon us.

Our futures were intertwined, woven together by loyalty and love. This was our pack, our family, our home. Thorin held no power here.

"Let's go," I declared, rising to my feet.

"You don't have to, I'll deal with him," he offered, his voice laced with concern as he took my hands, pressing them to his lips. I wasn't sure if I would ever grow accustomed to this softer side of him, but I offered him a smile, pulling him up from the couch.

"We face it together," I reminded him, our bond unbreakable. He sighed, nodding in agreement, and locked his hand in mine as we made our way to the entrance.

Stepping outside, I was met with the familiar sight of my father, his eyes immediately drawn to our interlocked hands.

"Hi, Dad."

"Ezra," he said, his gaze hardening as he took in the scene. "You're taking in mutts now, are you?"

He laughed at his joke, and the sound was grating like nails on a chalkboard. "You've changed," he added, looking over my appearance.

"Oh? In what way?"

"You look less…fragile."

"She was never fragile, simply mistreated and undervalued," Juno spoke at my side, and I smiled up at him.

My father scoffed. "So, it's true? My daughter married Junior Black?" my father asked, his disappointment ringing clear in his tone.

"What do you want?" I asked.

"I've come to offer my congratulations," he stated matter-of-factly.

"For?" I asked, slightly annoyed. "Clearly this isn't to congratulate me on my marriage."

"I've heard that I'm going to be a papa."

I looked at Juno. *How had he found out?* We've barely wrapped our heads around it, yet somehow, our enemies were aware?

Junior's thoughts mirrored my own. We had a leak. There was a traitor among us. He stepped in front of me, his wolf breaking through slightly in a protective stance.

"Are you alone?" I asked.

"I'm not a fool," he responded.

"That's debatable," I muttered under my breath.

"This is no concern of yours, Thorin." Junior spoke with a voice as cold as winter's breath.

But Thorin's presence was like a dark cloud, heavy with unspoken intentions. His sharp and unyielding eyes bore into mine as he spoke.

"Has your husband told you of his true intentions?"

A deep growl rumbled from Junior's chest, his eyes flashing with a dangerous light. "I intend to protect my family and ensure their safety," he said, his voice steady and firm.

Thorin's lips curled into a sneer. "Is that so? But that's not the whole truth, is it?"

I watched Junior's posture tighten. His hand was gripping mine tighter, like he was afraid he'd lose me. He was rattled. *What did my father know that I didn't?*

"You always did enjoy your games, boy," Thorin chuckled darkly, "but time is a luxury, and yours is running out. This game is nearly over, and in the end, you will lose."

My heart pounded in my chest as I glanced at Junior, searching his eyes for answers. He turned to me, his expression softening, but there was a shadow of worry behind his gaze. "I will tell you everything, Ezra. I promise. But you were never in danger. Not with me."

That familiar shiver crept down my back. Just a few minutes ago, it felt like we could get through anything together. Like no matter how crazy things got, we had this special place where nothing could touch us. Now? I wasn't so sure anymore.

Whatever Junior was hiding couldn't be good. But when I looked in his eyes, I saw something real. Despite the worry I knew he felt, I needed to trust him for us and Ayanna.

Thorin's eyes narrowed. "Remember, Ezra, trust is a fragile thing. Be careful who you place it in."

"Oh, that's rich coming from you," I sneered.

With that, he turned and walked away, leaving a heavy silence in his wake. I looked at Junior, my heart aching with a mix of love and uncertainty. "What was that all about?"

Junior pulled me close, his embrace warm and reassuring. "I think it's time I told you everything."

CHAPTER NINETEEN

I'm Not Sure He Isn't the Devil

Juno's POV

"I know I said I would explain everything to you, but I don't know how. I don't know where to start."

"Maybe try the beginning," she said, frustration evident in her tone. The slight bend of her knee, her hand resting against her full hips, told me I wasn't able to avoid this conversation any longer. I'd spent the last week dodging her questions, but she's given me more leniency than I deserved at this point. If you'd asked me a month ago if I'd be at the mercy of a feisty eighteen-year-old redhead, I would've laughed it off.

Yet here I was, about to bare my soul, terrified it would be the end of us. The stress of it had left me feeling nauseous. What if my confession was unforgivable? What if she walked away? I had only just got her back, and I wasn't sure I could live in this world without her now.

It wasn't that I didn't want her to know the truth behind why I took her as my Luna. She deserved that much. After everything we'd both gone through to get to this point, I knew she did. Yet, I couldn't find the words. Deep down, I think I knew from our very first interaction, I needed her. But I let my wounded pride destroy us before we ever began. How do I explain that?

Well, you see. The thing is, you were promised to me when you were eight. I, being thoroughly fucked up in the head, had agreed to the union because you were so innocent and pure. Somehow, even at eight, you were striking with your curly, red locks and icy-blue eyes, and I felt a pull toward you. Until your asshole father ended your mother and stole you from me.

I was so angry that he had crossed me, I vowed to get you back. I made it my life's mission to use you to ruin him, but somewhere along the way, things changed. I saw you grow into this incredible, strong woman, and my intentions shifted. It wasn't about revenge anymore. It was about love, about needing you by my side. I know it sounds twisted, but you became my light in the darkness.

Yeah, that sounded like shit.

"If that's your speech, you might as well throw in the towel now." Kai laughed.

"Not helping," I scolded him.

"Tell her everything. Your hate for him goes deeper than his crossing you. He stole someone you loved. Someone you both loved."

There was so much more to our story, and I wasn't sure she was ready to hear any of it, but the silence growing as I collected my thoughts was weighted, threatening to tear apart everything we've built.

"Ez?" I began gently. "Do you remember when I told you your mother tried to leave Night Tree Pack?" I asked.

"Yeah? You said she tried to take me with her."

I could see that bringing up Lina had caught her off guard. I hated seeing her cry more than anything, and I hoped, for both our sakes, that it wouldn't come to that. But if there was any chance for honesty, she needed the whole story. Even if it meant delving into a topic that caused both of us immense pain. Our shared past played such a vital role in where we stand today.

"Your mom came to me, terrified and desperate. She told me Thorin had done something unforgivable to you. She needed to keep you safe."

"Why are you telling me this?" she asked, her voice trembling.

I took a deep breath, knowing the hardest words had not yet come. "Because you deserve to know the truth, Ez. This is the beginning. She was willing to risk everything for you. She loved you more than anything in this world."

Ezra's eyes filled with tears, but she held them back, her voice barely above a whisper. "I don't understand. Why didn't she take me away? Why did she leave me there with him?"

"She tried, Ez. She really did. But your dad, uh, Thorin found out. He made sure she couldn't leave with you," I said, my heart aching with the weight of the truth. "I'm so sorry I couldn't save her. I tried; I really did try. But Ez, I think he killed her."

Ezra looked away, her shoulders trembling. "What? Why the fuck would you say that?! No. She left me. My dad said…"

She froze mid-sentence, turning back toward me. I watched as her eyes glossed over, and I immediately regretted this whole damned conversation. I broke her. I fucking shattered the one person in this life I cherished above all else. The one person I dared to feel anything for, since her mother.

I stepped closer to her, pulling her into my embrace. My voice soft, but firm. "Talk to me. Please, I'm sorry. I shouldn't have…Fuck, you weren't ready to hear any of this."

"Why?" she demanded. "Why do you think he killed her?"

Taking a deep breath, I reluctantly continued, "Lina was from my pack originally. If she were gonna leave, it's the only place she'd go. Her parents were from my pack. She wanted to get you far away from him, and her home pack would've been the safest place for you both. I'd never seen her wrecked like that. I knew your mom all my life, and she meant a great deal to me. She was the reason I made it through after my mom's death."

Ezra looked up at me, but said nothing. It was as if she were putting pieces of a puzzle together inside her mind, but she wasn't crying. *Was that a good sign?* I pulled her into my lap. "Do you want me to stop?"

"No. I...I'm sorry about your mom; I didn't know you lost her. How did it..."

"Cancer. She battled it for years, and I watched it take everything from her until there was nothing left. I was holding her hand when she passed. I had completely shut down for a while."

"Juno..."

"When she died, Dad rushed everything; the funeral was literally the next day, and after? That was it. We weren't supposed to talk about her. *'People die, life goes on, what's done is done, son',* my dad had said. He changed after that. He was so cold. I think when she died, he lost the best part of himself. I wouldn't have made it through, but your mom was there for me."

"I want to know everything you know about her...what was she like then?"

It was no secret; her mother held a special place in my heart. She offered me hope when it felt like there wasn't any. I was a troubled kid, so full of anger, who essentially lost two parents when my mother died, but she never gave up on me. When she told me she was leaving our pack, somehow that hurt more.

"When your mother was younger, she had a spirit that could light up the darkest nights. Her laughter was infectious, filling the air and everyone around her with joy and warmth. She had this unique way of seeing the world, with a curiosity and kindness that set her apart from everyone else. She was beautiful, but it was a beauty that lived within and radiated outward. When I look at you, I see that same spark, that same light. You remind me so much of her; it's as if her essence lives on in you."

"Do I look like her? My mother?" she asked.

I smiled softly. "Yes, Ezra, you do. You have her eyes, those same captivating eyes that seem to hold a world of stories. And your smile—it's just like hers, bright and full of life."

"Thank you," she whispered. "The way you talk about her…you really cared about her, didn't you?"

I took a deep breath, not knowing how she'd react to my answer, "Yes. I did. She was five years older. I was only thirteen when she announced she was pregnant and leaving our pack to be with your father. But she was the only woman I had ever thought I loved…until you."

"Wait…what?"

Shit. Did I ruin the first *I love you*, I'd ever said to a woman by telling her I loved her mother first? What in the shit was wrong with me?

"*Smooth*," Kai butted in.

"*Oh, fuck you.*"

"Dolly, I…"

"No. Nope. We aren't doing that right now…finish the story."

"Alright," I said softly, "your mother was determined to get you away from Thorin because she knew what he was capable of. She came to me because she trusted me, and she knew I'd do anything to help her…"

"Yeah, because you *loved* her."

"*Yes*, I did. But it wasn't the same. The way I love you? It's different. I've never felt like this about anyone."

"Seriously? My mother? What are you doing, just keeping it in the family? Or am I some consolation prize because you couldn't have her?"

"*Ouch.*" Kai laughed.

"No…it's nothing like that. I never meant to love you."

"Oh, so you regret falling for me?"

"That's not what I said…"

How had this gone from bad to worse so quickly?

"No, what you said was…"

"EZRA, SHUT UP AND FUCKING LISTEN TO ME!" My voice wasn't raised, but the steel in it brooked no argument. Her mouth opened, then snapped shut, an eye roll her only rebellion as she yielded the floor. "You're putting words in my mouth. Can you just be quiet and let me explain?"

I paused, waiting for her rebuttal that never came. "I never meant to fall for you, but I did. Not because you look like your mother, but because you are the strongest person I've ever met. I'm in awe of you, Ezra. I'm also so goddamn possessive of you, and I can't control this desire to destroy everything and everyone who has ever wronged you. I told you I cared about you profoundly, and what I should have said was that I loved you. You should never have heard it this way."

I wanted to touch her, pull her into me, and kiss this whole conversation into our history because I couldn't imagine a future without her in it. Maybe this went catastrophic because loving someone was so unfamiliar to me, or perhaps I just lost all common sense when looking into those eyes. But I was worried that the worst had come, and I would never be able to fix this now.

"Juno…I," she began, but I put my hand over her pretty mouth, stopping her mid-sentence. I needed to get this all out before I couldn't.

"Let me finish. Your mother and I were set to meet in neutral territory, the area around the college, where you chased me to the day I first tried to explain all this."

Ezra's eyes were wide, her breath shallow. "But?"

"She never showed, and I thought something terrible had happened, but I couldn't enter your pack territory. I later received a letter from her, asking me to meet up. She wanted me to take you with me. When I went to meet her, she wasn't there, but Thorin was."

"You think he'd kill her? Just because she wanted to leave?"

"It's more than that," I explained, my voice heavy with sorrow. "I think Thorin saw her as a threat. She knew too much about him; about the things he'd done. If she had left and told others, it could have ruined him. His empire would have fallen, and he couldn't let that happen. So, I think he made sure she couldn't escape by silencing her forever."

Ezra's fists clenched in my shirt, a mix of anger and grief in her eyes. "It was my fault."

"No, Ez. You were just a kid. It wasn't your fault."

"Yes, it was. He warned me, but I had blocked it out. I buried those memories deep so they couldn't hurt me anymore, but he had told me…if I weren't a good girl, he'd make sure mommy never woke up."

"Dolly…what happened?"

"He…they would fight. Mom always told me to hide, but eventually the shouting would end, and she'd be sleeping in their room. I wasn't allowed in, sometimes she'd sleep for days…"

She swallowed hard before starting again, tears staining her cheeks now. I reached forward, wiping them with my thumb as I cradled her face in my hands, pressing my forehead to hers.

"I tried to run away, but he caught me, I was screaming as he…" She shook her head; she didn't need to say the words. I knew. I knew what he had done. Lina never said, but I think in the darkest part of my mind, I had always suspected it. I pulled her so close I thought I might break her. Knowing this was her past made my hate for Thorin burn through me as my little one melted into me. As the memories washed over her, my thoughts raced.

What did that make me? Was I any better than that slimy fuck? I had essentially done the same thing. Sure, she enjoyed every goddamn minute of it, but…

I wanted her. I wanted her in a way I couldn't control.

"When I…that first night. You know you were always safe with me, right?"

"I know," she half-smiled at me. "You didn't hurt me, Juno. I was…already broken. What you did that night, I wanted it. I didn't know it at the time, but I did want it, and I wanted you. That was the first time I felt something other than blinding rage and sadness; it reminded me that I was still living."

"I've never been great with words, dolly. I might not always say the right thing, but I promise my love for you is real. I'd face the devil himself, if I had to, to keep you safe."

"I'm not sure he isn't the devil," she whispered, her voice trembling. "I hate him for what he did to her, to us."

I held her tighter, my heart breaking for her. "I know, Ez. I know, and trust me, he's dead; he'll pay his dues for all the ways he's wronged you. We'll end him together, cause when you don't feel strong enough on your own, you'll have me. It doesn't matter what life throws our way. We face it together."

"I know," she said through her cries.

"I am so proud to call you my wife," I said, stroking her cheek softly. "I will always protect you and our child, though my methods may be as dark as the night itself, sometimes. And yes, at times I may pull you into the abyss with me, but I will always ensure that darkness never touches you. I will be your shield, no matter what we face."

"I still don't…understand one thing. What were your intentions? Juno, why did you marry me?"

"That night, Thorin had crossed me in more ways than one, Ezra. He took you and your mother from me, and then he ostracized my pack. He spat in my face and told me I'd never have you. I wasn't much older than you are now, and if I could take it back, I would. Somewhere, along the way, something changed…you made me feel things I'd never felt before."

"You love me," she teased, sniffling.

"Yes, I love you, little one."

She leaned forward, and a massive part of me wanted to lean into that kiss, to get lost in the essence of everything she was to me. It would have been easy, but I couldn't, not before I told her everything. I needed to say the words I had been dreading. I pulled away, and she leaned back, clearly confused.

No, dolly, you did not misread that moment. I want to kiss you. I want to live, breathe, and die in the sweetness of your kisses, but…

"I swore I'd get you back, and when I did, I'd get my revenge on your father by making him watch as I ruined you, Ez. I went into this marriage with the intent of using you to break him. I wanted to take the most important thing in his life and destroy it. Just as he had done to me."

Ezra's eyes widened, and she slid off my lap, out of my arms, and it felt like my entire world had just slipped through my fingertips. She took a step back, her face a mixture of shock and betrayal.

"You...you wanted to ruin me? As in...kill me?" Her voice was barely a whisper, trembling with the weight of the revelation.

"Yes," I admitted, my heart aching with the truth. She had never deserved any of this, and the second I realized what she meant to me, my intent had shifted. "That was my plan. I was consumed by anger and hatred. I wanted to destroy him, and I thought the only way to do that was through you. But, Ezra, you have to understand—"

"Understand what?" she interrupted, tears streaming down her cheeks. "That you married me out of revenge? That you used me as a pawn in your twisted game?"

I reached out, desperate to make her see. "Ez, please, listen to me. That was how it started, but it's not how it ended. You changed me. You made me see that there was more to life than vengeance. You brought light into my darkness. I fell in love with you, truly and deeply. And now, all I want is to protect you, to be with you."

She shook her head, stepping further away. "How can I believe you? How can I trust anything you say after this?"

"Because I'm standing here, telling you the truth, knowing full well that it might cost me everything," I said, my voice breaking. "I'm baring my soul to you because you deserve to know everything. I don't want to hide anything from you. I can't, not anymore. I want nobody but you, Ezra. I want us, our family…"

Ezra stood there, looking torn between the love she might have felt for me and the pain of my betrayal. Finally, she spoke, her voice soft but resolute. "I need time, Juno. Time to process this, to figure out what it all means."

I nodded, understanding the gravity of her words. "Take all the time you need. I'll be here, waiting, ready to show you that my love is real."

Chapter Twenty

"Hormones"

Ezra's POV

As I strolled into the dining hall, I immediately saw Beth and Kit in line for dinner. They were deep in conversation and didn't seem to notice my approach.

"Are Mommy and Daddy fighting?" Beth asked Kit.

"I heard that," I muttered, stepping into line with them. I grabbed my plate, and immediately my nose scrunched up as my stomach began to turn. The scent of the chicken stir-fry hit me, and I cupped my mouth, trying to keep my stomach in check.

"What the heck is wrong with this kid? Stir-fry, too? I'm gonna starve to death at the rate she's going."

"Oh, Ezzie. It's okay, we ordered you a salad, you know, just in case," Kit assured me, rubbing my back.

"What would I do without you guys?" I asked, resting my head against her shoulder.

"Starve to death, clearly." Beth laughed.

"It's not funny, I love stir-fry," I grumbled. "Honestly, I just miss food so much," I whined.

Pulling me into a side hug, Kit said, "I'm just happy to see you. I really miss you, Ezzie."

"I'm happy to see you, too," Beth chimed in. "Now you can answer the question."

"I'm *fine*, Juno's *fine*, everything is just…"

"Fine?" asked Kit. "Yeah, we got it."

"We also know that's bullshit. So, spill it," Beth demanded, which had Kit giving her a *what the fuck?* look.

"What? You want to know, too."

Kit looked at me, back to her zero-fucks-given self. "I mean, she isn't wrong. A couple weeks ago, Junior literally kissed you in front of everyone."

"*And* carried you out of training. And now, when you see him, you avoid looking at him or make an excuse to leave. Talk to us."

"I'm just tired and, honestly, so irritated that my dad showed his face here. I promise, your "Mommy and Daddy" are fine."

It wasn't a lie; I was tired as hell. Who knew making a baby, especially in the first trimester, would be so hard? I was always sick. It was exhausting, and if Ayanna didn't get her shit together, I was gonna lose mine. On top of that, I had an ultrasound next week, and the whole thing was stressing me out. It should give us a more accurate estimation of how far along I was and an estimated due date.

Which meant I would soon know if this was Bash or Juno's baby. I wasn't sure I was ready to deal with that news. Right now, I wasn't even sure how to deal with everything Junior's little confession had brought with it.

I knew we both had our reasons for this marriage. It's not like I married him because I loved him. I don't think either one of us expected this—whatever it was—to happen between us. It's just that I didn't know how to trust him now.

I married him so that we could save our packs, his and mine. He married me so that he could use me to destroy my dad. Given everything he had told me, it seems my dad didn't just ruin my life, but Junior's, too.

So, was it fair to be upset about that? I hated that man with every fiber of my being, and that hatred burned hotter than ever after confronting the very real possibility that my dad had murdered my mother.

Given what Mom had meant to Juno…I could almost understand why he would go as far as he did to get his revenge. But I was beginning to picture this whole future with a man who not only loved my mother, which was cringey in its own right, but had also vowed to destroy me. That betrayal made me feel…foolish.

Still, I couldn't help the longing for him, or the void I felt now, without him near.

"What *did* Thorin want?" Kit asked, breaking the silence. I hadn't seen her much since the incident with Thorin. In my avoidance of Juno, everyone else got equal punishment, as we were all usually gathered in the same areas.

She knew he had come here last week; everyone did. The briefing the following morning included this information, but it was vague, as the only real thing he accomplished was putting a wedge between Juno and me.

It wouldn't do the pack any good to know that we were currently at odds with each other. He had also inadvertently let us know that we had a rat among us. So, it was better not to share too many details until we were able to weed them out.

"I'm sure Gabe sent him. It's hard to say what he wanted, though. All he did was insult my choice of husbands. Which I'll admit, gave me some satisfaction." I laughed.

I wished I could tell her the whole truth. I trusted this girl explicitly, but the traitor could be anyone, and we were currently in a very public dining hall, so this was all I could really say.

"Speaking of your husband." Beth's words cut through the air, nudging my line of sight forward. I tracked her gaze and spotted Junior heading my way.

"Wow, I am so full. Can't eat another bite. I'll see you all later," I blurted, scrambling up from the table. I bolted, but he was faster. *Curse his long legs.*

"This isn't about us," he said softly, taking my hand and guiding me out of the dining hall. Once outside, I wrenched my hand away. I wouldn't cause a scene in front of the pack, but out here, it was a different matter.

"Okay, so talk."

"I want to go to the baby appointment with you."

"Seriously, Juno? You said this wasn't about us."

"It isn't about us; it's about our baby."

"You don't know…"

"Yes, I know…biologically, there's a chance that little nugget isn't mine. Ez, I'm still your husband. I will be a good dad to them, no matter what bloodline they're from. His, mine, it doesn't matter. If you don't want me there, I'll respect your decision. But I needed you to know that I *want* to be there."

"Fine. Come if you want to."

"Thank you."

"This doesn't change anything. I don't trust you."

"Duly noted. But you will again, I'll prove myself; you'll see."

"I guess we will. Is that it, or is there more?" I asked. If I were stuck looking into those hazel eyes for one more minute, I was going to lose all my wits and kiss this man, and I wasn't ready to go there.

As if he could read my mind, he turned on his usual charm then, leaning forward, his familiar scent filling my nose…his eyes sparkling as he ran his hands down my arms. "Do you want there to be more?"

Damn. This. Man.

"*Always so stubborn, just forgive him…so you can ravage him already,*" Lana urged.

"*Quit being such a sex pest.*"

"*I feel what you feel, and you feel…*"

"*I know what I feel. Thank you very much.*"

"I…uh." His hand dipped into my lower back as his other hand cupped my cheek…and my mind was everywhere except where I wanted it to be. "When did you know?" I blurted out.

His voice deepened as he leaned forward. And something in his tone was intoxicating when he whispered, "When did I know what, dolly?" His words were rolling off his tongue, drawing me closer with each carefully spoken syllable, caressed with intent.

This man was everything I desired, and I was foolish and helpless against his pull. His breath brushed against my lips, enveloping my senses…the only thing missing was the taste of him. As I lost my breath, I began searching for it in all that he was. I could already feel the wetness pooling between my legs.

"That you loved me?" I managed to force out, between sharp bursts of breath. His hand moved to my throat and nudged my head back, his thumb pushing my jaw to the side. I gasped in anticipation. My neck was exposed to him, and my hands fisted the back of his shirt as I pulled his body closer, leaving no space between us.

A hungry growl escaped him as he gently bit and prodded my earlobe, his breath hot in my ear as his tongue flicked and teased before moving to my neck. The soft kiss he pressed there…undid me. A moan escaped, just as the doors behind us burst open. Horrified…I jumped back, and Juno, in his usual cocky form, chuckled.

"Okay, maybe Mom and Dad are just fine." Beth laughed.

Oh my Goddess.

I was seconds away from begging him to take me right here in the hallway. Kit and Zayne were with her…and both their jaws were on the floor.

"Don't look at me like that, blame the baby," I said, turning and quickly rushing down the hall.

"Hormones." Beth laughed.

There was a pause…a brief silence before Kit's voice echoed down the corridor. "Don't you even think about it."

I moved down the hall as quickly as my feet could carry me. But I was envisioning the look on Zayne's face that had provoked that response from her. And a playful smirk pulled at the corners of my mouth.

"Seriously? Hormones?" I muttered to myself, shaking my head. I was embarrassed and confused, but my friends definitely kept things interesting.

It was true, though. Everything felt amplified. Smells were stronger, sounds were sharper, and my emotions? Trying to understand them was lost on me.

I was still so mad at Junior, but the way he touched me…had skipped my brain entirely, detouring straight to my aching pussy. I would never be able to forget what he felt like, and I wanted that feeling again. So much so, it was almost painful. I was helplessly aware of just how much I had missed him, and I hated him for it.

The thrill of that shared moment with Junior lingered, an intoxicating hum like the echo of a beautiful song. I turned down the corridor leading to the living quarters and leaned against the wall, trying to catch my breath. My fingers traced over the spots where his touch still lingered, the laughter of my friends trailing behind me like a distant melody.

When I heard footsteps approaching, my pulse quickened again, my hands dropping to my sides. Had Juno followed me? *Did I want him to follow me?*

Zayne appeared suddenly, a teasing smirk on his face. "You do know, if you keep running away like that, I'm gonna have to start taking cardio seriously. Just so I can chase you down." His voice was low and playful, and I was relieved to see him rounding that corner.

"I'm sorry, Zayne. I think I was just a little embarrassed."

"Don't be. Look, if it makes you happy being with him, then I say go for it. I mean, I may not always like him, but I think his feelings for you are genuine."

"Maybe…but it didn't start that way, Zayne. I'm not sure how to really feel right now. My head, my heart, and my… desire won't get on the same page these days."

"What do you mean? You two seemed fine back there." He laughed, pointing down the hall.

"Shut up! Please don't remind me. Actually, I'm glad you walked in on us, or out on us? Whatever, I'm glad it stopped there."

"Okay, come on. Talk to me. No more secrets, yeah?"

"I don't know. It's like my head is giving me all these reasons not to trust him, while my heart…Zayne, I thought I had lost it. Turns out, it was only in hibernation, and now that it's awakened, it only wants to beat for him and his stupid, perfectly chiseled biceps."

"Okay, I really didn't need the mental image of Junior's arms in my head, although I'll admit, the guy *is* stacked. But I'm more interested in why your head won't let you trust him, Ezzie."

"Kit's rubbing off on you."

"Yeah, well. I really like that nickname, it suits you."

I sighed, pulling my knees to my chest and hugging them tightly, feeling the weight of my conflicting emotions pressing down on me. "It's just...Junior kept all these secrets from me, Zayne. Our history is way more complicated than I had realized. There are all these shadows lurking in all the secrets he's kept, and my head is screaming at me to protect myself."

Zayne leaned back against the wall, his expression thoughtful. "Secrets can be heavy, Ezzie. But sometimes, people carry them because they're afraid of what others might think, or how it might change things. Have you tried talking to him about it? Really talking?"

I bit my lip, considering his words. We had talked. I even understood why he would be afraid to tell me. Still, he knew the whole time about what my father had done. He knew, and he kept that from me. When this began, I was nothing more than a pawn in a game I never consented to play.

I think the most frustrating part was that his entire plan just didn't make any sense to me. I meant absolutely nothing to my dad. How would that even begin to get him his revenge? My dad has hated me my entire life.

My pain? My very existence? Meant nothing to that man.

"We talked. But Zayne, it still feels like there are so many secrets between us. It makes me wonder if it will always be that way. It's like he's built a fortress around his heart, and I can't find a way in."

Zayne reached out, gently squeezing my hand. "Give him time, Ezzie. Walls are usually built to shield us from pain, and some take more time to break down than others. If I remember correctly, yours used to be quite high, too."

"Sometimes, it feels like they always will be."

"Just…whatever you decide, trust your instincts. Unless they are telling you to run away—please fight those, because I really hate running."

"I'll try. I honestly don't know why I always run away."

I leaned my head against his shoulder, and in true Zayne fashion, he just sat with me. This kid was always joking around, but he was actually so easy to talk to. His advice was always pretty solid, too. Who knew there was so much hidden beneath the surface?

"Should we talk about you and Kit, now?" I teased, playfully jabbing him with my elbow.

"Well, I know one thing for sure. We will not be having any babies in the near future." He laughed, and his laughter was infectious.

As the laughter died down and the silence once again fell over us, Zayne looked down at me. Not a hint of humor left in his voice. "I think I'd be a good dad, though. You know, someday."

"Yes. Without a doubt, you are heading for paternal greatness."

CHAPTER TWENTY-ONE
Just Name It and It's Yours

Juno's POV

Snowflakes illuminated under the streetlights below. From my office nook, I watched the city snow globe, lost in a thought I couldn't shake. Regret? Nope, not a chance. Having her in my arms felt less like a choice and more like gravity finally working as intended.

Our paths were always meant to cross. That was inevitable—an unalterable truth, etched into the cosmos like constellations guiding lost travelers. All I knew for sure was I couldn't live without her, not in this moment, not in any future. To let her go would be to unravel a part of myself, to extinguish a light that had finally found its way home.

Admittedly, putting moves on Ezra in the hallway may not have been my finest moment. After unloading all my baggage, she probably needed breathing room, not a surprise attack. If she had pulled away, maybe I could have given her that, temporarily, but she didn't. Those hands gripping my shirt, her leaning in—undid me.

The pull was undeniable. I was beginning to wonder if this intense hunger was mine or my wolf, Kai's. Whatever the case, locking eyes with Ezra turned my willpower into a puddle. I wanted to be near her. No, I *needed* to be near her again, pure and simple.

The memory of that moment with her was a constant distraction. I had to fully immerse myself in war planning in order to restrain myself, and I had a plan, mostly. We're not sitting ducks anymore; our recruits are ready. We've got the numbers, and the first strike could give us an edge. The only glitch in my grand plan? Keeping Ezra safe and sound on the sidelines.

Her stubbornness was a storm, and she had a strange talent for dancing on the edge of danger. She was all impulse, a spark without a plan. It was maddening trying to protect her when she seemed to have no instinct for self-preservation.

The knock on the door caused me to pause as it opened.

Ezra.

Lost in the intoxicating pull of her, I forgot the careful boundaries I'd sworn to respect. The scent of her—wild berries and something uniquely hers—drove Kai into a frenzy, blurring the line between our desires. Releasing the curtains, I closed the space between us.

"Can we talk?" she asked, closing the door securely behind her, leaning against it.

"Anything you need, just name it and it's yours." I held my hand out, and she allowed me to take it, leading us to the sitting area. She didn't speak for a long while, and the anticipation was killing me.

"When did it change? Your plan," she asked, a hint of confusion in her voice.

I paused, considering the question. "If you're searching for one specific moment, I can't give you one. Perhaps it was when I realized I couldn't bear seeing those tears in your eyes, or maybe it was the way you carried yourself after that night in the dining hall. Or even the fire in your voice, when you spoke out against me, fearless and strong."

Softening my voice, I continued, "The night I found you nearly frozen on the ground, I caught a glimpse of what it would feel like to lose you. To really lose you, and I think I knew then I couldn't bring myself to hurt you. And when I saw that wolf from Silver pack put his hands on you, I lost my mind. I didn't care about anything besides making him pay."

"I can't tell you exactly when," I repeated, staring at her intensely. "And if I were to explain why, the reasons would be endless, but they can also be summed up with four words: because I love you." I leaned into her, but she mirrored my movement, creating this distance between us that felt vast and uncertain.

Was this the moment I've been dreading? Was I about to lose her? *Shit.* I kneeled before her, but she refused to look into my eyes.

What's the right play here?

Do I put myself at her mercy?

Do I beg?

Before I could question it, I was pulling her face to mine, and as our lips met, I could feel her hesitation. It was a silent plea, a desperate call for reassurance. I pulled back, just enough to see her face and the conflict etched in every line.

"Ezra," I murmured, my voice rough with need and regret. "I'm sorry. I didn't mean to push."

My hand reached up to cup her cheek, my thumb gently stroking her soft skin. "I just...can't seem to stay away from you."

I watched as she struggled to hold back the tears, her eyes wide and glossy. I saw the quiver in her bottom lip as she sharply inhaled each breath. And as a flicker of hesitation crossed her eyes, that subtle tremor sliced through my haze—saying more than words ever could.

I realized in that moment exactly how much Ezra meant to me. Her pain was a mirror to my own, and I refused to be its cause. To truly love her demanded sacrifice—releasing her from my grasp, even as my heart shattered into a million pieces. It was about cherishing her well-being above my desires, a bittersweet surrender for her sake.

Ezra's POV

The vulnerability in his gaze was going to be my undoing. "Tell me what you need," he whispered, resting his forehead against mine. "Tell me, and I'll give it to you, even if it means walking away."

My heart clenched at his words, each syllable a hammer blow against the fragile hope I'd been harboring that somehow, this was going to be an easy decision. "I just… can't," I managed to choke out, my voice thick with tears. "Whatever this is, or was…it needs to end here."

I watched as the words, sharp and final, left my lips, each syllable a tiny shard of glass piercing the tender fabric of our shared connection. He didn't argue, didn't plead. But the way his head tilted back, the way his eyes closed against the sting of my words had left me questioning what I had just done.

Honestly, I wasn't sure which way this conversation was going to go when I walked in here. I spent the last week wishing we could go back and just live in the perfect little bubble we'd created that day in the library. I wanted to forgive him and to believe in the vision Selene had given me of our future with Ayanna. But I couldn't. I just didn't trust him anymore, and I wasn't sure if I ever would again.

"I understand," he finally managed, his voice a strained whisper. The admission felt like he was surrendering a vital part of himself.

Slowly, he lowered his hand from my cheek, the warmth of his touch fading from my skin. "Then I'll walk away," he said, the words heavy with the weight of a thousand unspoken goodbyes. "I'll give you the space you need, even if it tears me apart."

With that, he took a step back, creating a physical distance that mirrored the space now separating our hearts. "Just know," he added, his gaze locked on mine, "if you ever change your mind, I will *always* be here, waiting for you."

As he turned to leave, the scent of his familiar cologne lingered in the air, stirring a bittersweet ache in my heart. The door clicked shut, and with it, the echo of a love story untold. I sank to the floor, the ticking of the clock now a mocking reminder of the relentless passage of time. Each second carrying us further away from the 'us' we were meant to be.

CHAPTER TWENTY-TWO

A Little Heart to Heart

Ezra's POV

Three days. It's been three days since we last spoke. Three damn days, and still, I can't bring myself to tell my friends about Juno and me. This was the perfect opportunity, yet the words remain trapped in my throat as the firelight crackles, casting shadows across their unsuspecting faces.

Luckily, Kit has never been at a loss for words. Raising her glass, she announced, "I just wanted to take a minute to say, I love you guys!"

Forcing a smile, I followed suit, raising my glass to a toast that felt like swallowing ash.

"You still love him."

It wasn't a question, but I answered my wolf anyway, *"Yes, Lana. You're probably right,"* before turning my attention back to my friends, giving a toast of my own.

"I know we've been through it for the past two months, but you're truly, without a doubt, the best friends anyone could ever ask for. I don't know where I'd be without you guys."

Kit draped an arm over my shoulders, squeezing me tight. "We're not just friends, Ezzie. We're family."

I leaned into her embrace, a warmth spreading through me. "A toast to family, then."

"To family!" The chorus echoed, and glasses were raised in unison before we all drank.

"Speaking of families, how's our little one doing?" Kit asked. "I'm honestly pissed Juno didn't come with you. But at least he released us early from training; we needed this."

"Yeah, he's been busy lately. I barely see him myself, and I'm sure she's fine." I smiled as I looked down at my belly.

"She?"

"It's just a feeling," I said, remembering Bash's declaration that she would be named Ayanna. This time, a genuine smile came.

"Well, let's not waste any time, let's make some memories, yeah?" Zayne shouted, his voice full of life as he turned the music up.

I sank onto the couch, watching as everyone erupted into laughter and celebration—a hollow ache forming in my chest.

It was Kit's idea to hang out tonight, and she was right. We all desperately needed to have some fun. It felt like a lifetime since any of us had hung out, and I genuinely missed these guys. But between training, Ayanna, and everything with Juno, I was exhausted.

As the night deepened, the library transformed into a sanctuary of warmth and love. We took turns telling stories, sharing memories, and inside jokes that only we understood. Zayne, ever the storyteller, recounted the tale of us fighting Gabriel, exaggerating the event with theatrical flair, earning roars of laughter from the group. Every time Kit and Zayne kissed, Beth and I shared a look of playful disgust that left us laughing hysterically.

Surrounded by my chosen family, I felt a sense of peace washing over me, but I couldn't help but wish that one last person had been present tonight. I sat there, staring into the heart of the fire, the crackling and popping fading as I drifted into my thoughts.

"Ezzie?" Kit began, her voice soft as she settled beside me on the couch, "How are you really doing? I know you, and I see the shadows in your eyes."

I sighed, leaning into her comforting presence. "It's just...the memories, Kit. They still haunt me sometimes."

"They always will, in some way," she murmured, "but they don't define you."

Before I could respond, the library doors burst open, and Junior strode in, followed by Alec and Nyx. Seeing him, a jolt went through me, and I instinctively sat up straighter. He looked…fuck, he looked so damn good, a dangerous allure radiating from him.

Junior grinned, his eyes sparkling with mischief. It was unsettling how easily he could revert to the "old" Juno, but now I could see right through the façade; a shadow lingered beneath the surface. Any hints of his vulnerability were carefully concealed, but I recognized the mask, the same one I wore for my friends.

I had tried to tear down his walls, and now they seemed higher, more impenetrable than ever. But beneath the surface, I could sense the pain. I felt that same ache within my own heart.

Alec raised an eyebrow. "Curfew was two hours ago, Luna."

"Oh no, it must be a rebellion," Beth teased, but the humor felt strained.

"I think you should all get to your rooms, it's late, and you're going to need your rest for tomorrow," Juno said, his voice a touch too casual as Nyx moved possessively beside him.

"He's got some nerve," Lana growled.

"I broke up with him, remember?" I reminded my wolf, but I'll admit. It hurt to see them together. *"I don't have the right to choose who he spends his time with, but I'm thinking I really should have told everyone, now."*

"Filthy lying, mutt. Declares he loves you, and moves on two seconds later."

"You don't know that, Lana. He said they were really good friends."

Sometimes I hated how strong-willed and blunt my wolf was. Not that she was wrong—it didn't make sense for him to show up here with her. Of course, the fact that I didn't trust him was why I ended things. Perhaps he was a better liar than I thought, and his so-called love was also a lie.

Nyx tilted her head; her gaze fixed upon me in careful study before feigning concern with a question. "Ezzie, are you alright? You seem somewhat...lost in thought."

Kit squeezed my hand reassuringly. "We're fine, Nyx. Just having a little heart-to-heart."

Her gaze flicked back to mine, a silent challenge passing between us as she spoke again. "Juno," she purred, her voice dripping with honeyed poison. "Let the kids play, and let's go to bed."

Her words were laced with venom, a subtle sting that only I seemed to notice, or so I thought. To my surprise, I watched Juno's jaw tighten, his knuckles turning white as he gripped his phone. Together or not, we were married. This was our pack.

"Let's go to bed? Are they sleeping together now?" I asked Lana.

"I will crush her, release me!"

"Lana…calm yourself."

"Do not cage me, child."

"We can't attack her for being a bitch, she's still a part of this pack."

"I don't trust her."

"Me neither. But if she wants a fight…"

"Actually," I said, standing up, meeting Nyx's gaze head-on, "I think you should join the 'kids' for a drink, while Juno and I head off to bed. You deserve to have some fun, too. And my husband and I have things to discuss."

Nyx's eyes narrowed, the honeyed sweetness vanishing, replaced by a glint of something sharp and dangerous. Juno's gaze flickered between us, and I wondered if this exchange looked as awkward as it felt to everyone else in the room.

I'd never been the jealous type, but this 'little sister' of his just kept rubbing me, and apparently, Lana, the wrong way. It was clear as day, she didn't see him the same way he saw her.

"Discuss?" Nyx finally echoed. "I wasn't aware there was anything between you two that required…discussion." She stepped closer to Juno, her hand sliding possessively around his arm, an explicit declaration of ownership.

Everyone in the room went silent. There was no hiding it now. Anyone with eyes would see that something wasn't right.

My gut clenched, maybe because of Nyx's action. But honestly, I think I felt more guilty for not telling the gang about our breakup sooner. I'd kept a lot of things from my friends in the past, and it wasn't like it was a secret. I wanted to tell them, but if I had spoken the words out loud, it would have made it true.

Juno's gaze fell upon Nyx's hand, a flicker of annoyance crossing his features before he gently disentangled himself from her grasp. "Nyx, please," he murmured, his voice laced with weariness. "You're not helping."

A shadow of hurt crossed Nyx's face, her eyes flashing with a wounded defiance. "It's never bothered you before," she retorted, her voice laced with a hint of bitterness.

Juno's expression hardened. "That's enough," he declared, his voice ringing with an undeniable finality that brooked no argument.

"There are always things to discuss, Nyx," I replied, my voice steady despite the tremor in my heart. "Especially when the truth is buried beneath layers of lies."

My gaze locked with Juno's, pleading with him as all eyes turned to him. He stood frozen, caught in the crossfire, his face a mask of carefully controlled neutrality. I had no right to ask this of him, especially after making it clear that we were done.

"Yeah," Juno finally said, his voice a low rumble that seemed to vibrate through the very ground beneath our feet. "Let's go have a chat."

He paused, his gaze sweeping from Nyx to me, a flicker of something unreadable in his eyes. "Luna," he said, his voice softening, "lead the way."

He waited patiently as I said my goodbyes. Nyx had abruptly stormed off, earning a grunt of satisfaction from Lana, while Alec made his way to Beth and the others. After a tight hug with Kit, I saw Alec greeting Zayne with what I'd call a bro hug, before I left with Juno. I actually didn't mind him so much; he had definitely grown on me over the past few months, and it seemed that he and Zayne got along pretty well.

As we walked down the hallway, my eyes couldn't help but steal glances his way. A whirlwind of thoughts swirled within me, each one a question mark hanging in the air. Should I bring up what happened? Or the ultrasound tomorrow? Or perhaps explain that I haven't told anyone about what happened between us?

"Like what you see, Luna?" he asked, nonchalantly as we entered the staircase leading upstairs.

"I'm sorry, it's just…" I began, but he stopped suddenly, turning to face me. "I was kidding," he said, arching his brow.

Playfully, I hit him. "I hate you."

A laugh escaped him as he continued up the stairs, the sound echoing in the stairwell, and I couldn't help but smile, too.

"Mhmm. So, what were you guys up to?"

"Just blowing off a bit of steam," I replied.

"You haven't told them, have you?" he asked, his eyes searching mine, as we entered the office.

"No. I haven't."

"You know they will find out eventually, and it's better if it comes from you, little one."

"Yeah. I know."

He paused, his expression shifting into a thoughtful mask, his eyes boring into mine. "Unless, of course, there's a reason why you haven't told them?"

"So, Nyx, huh?" I countered, trying to steer the conversation elsewhere.

"She was out of line," he stated, a dismissive wave of his hand accompanying the words.

"Do you love her?"

"*What?!*" he responded, surprise evident in his voice.

"It's okay, you have the right to date whoever you want," I said, keeping my voice as steady as I could, though my heart fluttered unsteadily in my chest.

"No, Ez. I don't love Nyx. Not the way I love you. You are the only person I will *ever* love."

My breath hitched in my throat, my thoughts scrambling to make sense of his words. I wasn't sure why I even asked him that in the first place, and now I wasn't sure how to respond to his answer. "I don't think she got the memo," I finally whispered, my gaze fixed on the space between us.

"Ezra…" he murmured, his voice laced with a tenderness that tugged at my resolve. He closed the distance, his hand gently finding my cheek, urging me to meet his eyes. "Don't you see? It has always been you. It will always be you."

Torn between the siren call of his words and the jagged edges of our past, I choked, "I don't know what to say, Juno. My heart aches, the scars you've left…they run deep."

"I know, little one. But beneath that, how do you feel?"

"I feel like I was a part of you, Juno. Like I was woven into the very fabric of your soul. And now I feel lost, I don't know how to find the me I was before you now."

His voice, a silken plea, cut through my turmoil. "No, Ezra. How do you feel about me, the man who stands before you, bared and vulnerable? Do you feel anything?"

I pulled away from his touch; the raw emotion of this was too much to bear. "Juno, please, don't ask me to answer that."

"Do you love me, Ezra Ken?"

I was fumbling for words. Grasping at straws that didn't exist, but I knew I couldn't answer that question. Telling him how I truly felt wouldn't change anything. We couldn't go back now, no matter how much I wished we could. "Are you coming to the appointment tomorrow?"

A flicker of pain crossed his face. "Don't deflect, Ezra. Don't hide from the truth."

"Are you coming or not?"

"Of course, I am! Did I not say I would?" As quickly as his anger flared, it subsided, his gaze softening with an almost painful tenderness. "The baby changes nothing about how I feel for you, Ezra. It's a part of us, a new chapter, but you are my story, from beginning to end. I only hope one day, you will see that. I will never stop hoping for it. Whether that day comes or not, I will be a good dad to our child. And I promise, I will never stop loving you."

A tear escaped, tracing a path down my cheek. "You're promises don't mean anything, Juno. Not anymore."

"And you can't deny how you feel."

In that moment, surrounded by the quiet of the office and the weight of his words, I knew that he was right. Whatever the future held, he would be a part of it, because yeah. I did love him, and he knew it. "Okay," I whispered, finally meeting his eyes. "I'll see you tomorrow night."

CHAPTER TWENTY-THREE

The Enforcers

Juno's POV

"Are you ready?" the nurse asked, her voice gentle as she squirted the warm jelly on Ezra's abdomen. We both nodded, a silent promise of support passing between us as I took her hand in mine. The air in the room began to mimic our nervous energy, thick with a mix of anticipation and excitement. "Okay, here we go," the nurse instructed us, her movements precise as she began moving the wand around, her eyes focused on the monitor.

"There we are, you see right here?" she asked, her tone laced with a hint of wonder as she pointed to the black-and-white image on the monitor. "There's your little one, there." She smiled, a warm, reassuring smile that eased some of the tension in the room.

"That's the baby? Are you sure?" I asked, my voice laced with disbelief, probably sounding like the most uneducated man on the planet. But in my defense, it didn't look like a baby. It looked like a bright peanut-shaped blob in a sea of black. The moment was—well, it was probably the most profound moment of my life. So good, I could almost trick myself into believing that everything was okay.

"Yes, Alpha. I'm sure. It's still very early in the pregnancy, so unfortunately, you'll have to wait to count fingers and toes." The nurse chuckled softly, her eyes crinkling at the corners.

"Can you tell?" Ezra asked, her voice barely above a whisper. "Can you tell how far along I am?" Her eyes were glued to the monitor, searching for any sign of the little life growing within her.

"I'm going to take some measurements, Luna, to help give us a better idea of the gestational age of the baby," the nurse assured her. Her touch was gentle as she adjusted the wand, capturing the precious images that would forever be etched in our memories.

I was secretly praying this child was mine, a silent plea echoing in the chambers of my heart. The feeling was overwhelming, gnawing at my insides, a conviction that fate had conspired to bring this child to my doorstep. *She was mine,* my soul whispered, staking its claim.

"This is…strange." The nurse's words hung in the air, her apology, a fleeting shadow, quickly replaced by concern as she excused herself.

"Do you think there is something wrong with her?" Ezra asked.

"Her?" I echoed. The question, laced with yearning, I dared not voice.

"Yeah, Ayanna. That's what I'm gonna name her. What do you think?"

"It could be a boy, you know," I replied, trying to temper the burgeoning hope in my heart.

"Maybe, but I have a feeling this little one is a girl," Ezra said with a knowing smile.

"We call that mother's intuition," the head nurse chimed in, her entrance accompanied by the ultrasound technician, their hushed tones a stark contrast to the joy Ezra radiated.

"Is everything okay?" I asked, a knot forming in my stomach as the nurses studied the images, their silence amplifying my fears.

"Oh, yes. I apologize; everything looks perfect. Except, well, I'm sorry to be awful blunt, Alpha Black, but you two have only been married for six weeks, correct?"

The head nurse's question was a jarring intrusion, shattering the delicate bubble of hope I had allowed myself to create. "Yes, ma'am. But Ezra was mated prior to our marriage," I answered, my voice barely a whisper, bracing myself for the revelation that was sure to follow.

"Oh, I see." She smiled at us both, almost apologetically. "Based on these measurements, I'd say it's more likely that you're about nine weeks pregnant, Luna."

Ezra remained a statue, her gaze fixed on the monitor, her silence a deafening roar in the small room. "Yes, we understand. Thank you, ma'am," I managed to utter, the words a hollow echo of composure masking the turmoil within. How I summoned the strength to speak, I couldn't tell you.

"Can we go now?" Ezra's voice was a mere whisper, devoid of its usual warmth, a stark testament to the shock that had seized her.

"Oh yes, of course," the head nurse replied, her voice laced with concern. "Let me just clean you up."

Her actions were gentle, but they couldn't erase the truth that had just been revealed, a truth that threatened to unravel the fragile tapestry of our newly formed union. The baby wasn't mine. I swore it wouldn't matter, but I hadn't fully prepared myself for the reality of it.

I watched Ezra stand; each adjustment of her clothing felt like the tightening of a noose around my heart. She grabbed her phone, the glint mirroring the cold finality of the moment. She quickly moved around the hospital bed, a brief, agonizing pause before me. Her eyes met mine for a fleeting second—an eternity. In that hesitation, the almost imperceptible parting of her lips, I saw the unspoken words, the confessions she dared not utter. It was the end, etched in the silence, as she walked out of the room, taking a piece of my soul with her.

I wanted to go after her, to hold her tightly in my embrace, whispering reassurances that this revelation held no weight, that it changed nothing. The words teetered on the edge of my tongue, desperate to be voiced. Yet, as I stood there, my gaze locked on the newly vacant doorway, her haunting expression seared into the depths of my mind.

A cruel whisper slithered into my thoughts: *perhaps, if that child were mine, she would have found her way back to me, drawn by the invisible threads of our shared creation.* But that child was his, her dead mate's, and I couldn't summon the conviction to believe such a reunion was possible now.

The sterile scent of the clinic seemed to amplify the emptiness she left behind. Each breath I took felt like a betrayal, a reminder of my vitality in contrast to my quiet despair. My feet felt rooted in place, as if the floor itself conspired against me. Keeping me from moving forward, from causing myself further pain by running after her.

I closed my eyes, in an attempt to conjure her image in my mind: the way her brow furrowed when she was angry, the soft curve of her lips when she smiled, that fire that danced in her eyes.

But now, all I could see was the shattered reflection of that fire, extinguished by the weight of circumstance. The dream I had woven together in my mind, a tapestry of hopes and intertwined futures, now seemed to fray at the edges, unravelling completely.

Against my better judgement and with a surge of determination, I managed to break free from my paralysis. I exited the room, propelled by the need to find her, to offer solace, to navigate this treacherous new terrain together. I would not let this unspoken truth become an insurmountable barrier. I would fight for our love, even if it meant facing the unknown with nothing but the fragile hope that, somehow, we could find our way back to each other.

The persistent ringing of my phone in my pocket felt like yet another intrusion. Impatient, I pulled it out and hurled it against the wall. The shattering plastic and scattering components echoed in the empty hall as I took off running toward the infirmary exit.

Bursting through the doors, I collided with Alec. The impact was jarring, but his hands were on my shoulders, keeping me upright. Zayne was beside him, blocking my escape.

"Move, Zayne. Whatever this is, it can wait."

"No, it can't."

"YES, IT CAN."

I tried to push past him, but Alec's words hung in the air, inescapable. "Junior, Thorin is here, and he isn't alone."

Those words were suspended in time, each syllable a stone sinking into the pit of my stomach. My breath hitched, the urgency that had propelled me moments ago now faltering, replaced by a chilling premonition. Thorin. Here. Not alone. The implications swirled like a tempest, threatening to capsize the fragile hope I clung to.

"What do you mean, he's not alone?" I managed, my voice a strained whisper. Alec's grip tightened on my shoulders, his eyes mirroring the gravity of the situation. "He's with the Enforcers, Juno. They're here for Ezra."

The world tilted on its axis—the Enforcers. The iron fist of Werewolf Authority had come with Thorin to claim what was mine. My heart hammered against my ribs, a frantic drumbeat against the encroaching dread.

This wasn't just about revenge or power anymore. This wasn't a war between packs; if they were involved, this was a battle for her freedom, her very life. "Where are they?" I demanded, my voice regaining its edge, the paralysis of fear now replaced by a fierce resolve. "Where is she?"

"They're outside," Alec said, his voice tight with urgency.

"And Ezra? Alec, *where* is she?"

Zayne answered through gritted teeth. "They have her."

"*They have her?*" I echoed his response as the anger surged through me. "But why? What could they possibly want with her?"

"I really don't know, but Juno, you need to be careful," Alec pleaded with me. "The Enforcers rarely get involved in pack disputes, and they don't mess around. I feel like we're missing something here. We need to be smart."

I shoved past Zayne and Alec, my mind racing. "*Careful* went out the window the moment they set foot on our grounds." I didn't break stride, my focus narrowing to a single point: getting to her. The infirmary was only a few corridors away from the main doors, but each step felt like a mile. My hands clenched into fists, nails digging into my palms.

Rounding the corner, I pushed through the large wooden doors to find the Enforcers, in their black uniforms, their faces grim and impassive, standing in formation. Thorin stood at the center, his eyes cold and calculating. She was being held by two men, behind him. I committed their faces to memory as my blood ran cold, then hot with fury. This was not how our story was supposed to go.

I strode forward. "One chance. You get one chance to release her, or I'll kill you where you stand, Thorin."

Thorin, wasting no time, declared, "This is out of our hands, now. I've only come to claim my grandchild. Ezra will not be harmed."

"Over my dead body," I warned.

"Your threats mean nothing. I will be leaving here with her and my grandchild." His voice was a thunderous echo of authority. "This child carries the legacy of our bloodline, a heritage that cannot be ignored."

As he spoke, the Enforcers placed iron shackles on Ezra. I watched as she strained against their hold on her. Zayne and Alec moved to my side, their presence a silent vow. No matter which way this went, they were willing to put their lives on the line right along with me.

Thorin's gaze shifted to the Enforcers. "These are no ordinary wolves, I'm sure you're aware," he murmured, almost to himself. "They are bound to the prophecy, as well."

The wolves holding Ezra began to drag her away, and Thorin turned on his heels following them. The remaining Enforcers tightened their formation, forming a protective wall between them and us.

"You will not be taking my WIFE anywhere!" I yelled.

The tension had reached a breaking point. Without a second thought, I charged—my momentum carrying me forward; a human missile aimed at the heart of the

Enforcers' formation. The first guy didn't have time to react, and I slammed into him with enough force to send him stumbling backward, disrupting their ranks.

"Juno, stop!" I heard Alec shout from behind, but I couldn't stop, wouldn't stop.

The Enforcers reacted quickly, their training kicking in. Two of them moved to intercept me, but I was already moving, weaving between them with a speed I didn't know I even possessed. Adrenaline coursed through my veins, sharpening my senses, amplifying my strength.

Thorin stepped forward, his expression unreadable as he pushed me back. "This doesn't have to end this way, Juno. Stand down, and no one else gets hurt."

Kai's growl echoed throughout the grounds, and Thorin's eyes narrowed, a dangerous glint flashing within them. Thorin lunged forward, shifting mid-flight as the Enforcers attacked on all sides.

While I was trying to recover my footing, I found myself struggling to keep Ezra in my line of sight. They were moving quickly, already at the bottom of the stairs, moving toward a large, unmarked vehicle. A movement to my right caught my attention. I turned, relief washing over me when I saw Dalton and all of Second Squad rounding the corner of the pack house. Reinforcements.

When Dalton's eyes landed on Ezra, he froze momentarily, his expression mirroring the thoughts in my head.

"GET HER," I ordered, while adrenaline surged through my veins, each command a burst of urgency.

Second Squad surged forward, their determination a palpable force as they sprinted towards the vehicle, but it was too late. I watched helplessly as Dalton reached out, his fingers grazed Ezra's sleeve, but she slipped through his grasp like smoke, an ethereal figure fading into the night. The vehicle's engine roared to life, its headlights cutting through the darkness as it sped away, carrying Ezra with it.

A wave of despair washed over me, a cold tide threatening to drown me in its depths. My knees buckled, and I sank to the ground, the weight of my failure crushing me.

Suddenly, I felt a jolt of electricity coursing through my body, sending me crashing face down on the pavement. As I struggled to maintain consciousness, I watched as one by one, my wolves fell. The Enforcers levelled us within minutes.

They had completed their mission. They took her, my little one, my Ezra. I promised I'd protect her, but the night had swallowed her whole, leaving me alone in the deafening silence of defeat.

CHAPTER TWENTY-FOUR
Creature of Legend

Ezra's POV

Confined within these cold, concrete walls, the truth crashed upon me like a tidal wave. It wasn't me they were after, but my unborn child. Ayanna would be a beacon of hope or a harbinger of doom; she held the fate of werewolf kind in her tiny hands, and I wasn't the only one who knew. *This child carries the legacy of our bloodline.* Those were the words Thorin had spoken.

The prophecy echoed in my mind, a relentless drumbeat of destiny. Light and dark, balanced on the precipice, hinged on the very existence of my child. I was nothing more than a vessel for a future I could barely comprehend.

A future as uncertain as the Enforcers' intentions. The holding cell was a symphony of despair; its concrete walls stained with shadows of forgotten souls. A single, flickering bulb cast long, dancing silhouettes, mocking the desolation that permeated every corner. The air was thick with the stench of stale fear and hopelessness that clung to the cold metal cot serving as my only refuge.

Suddenly, the heavy door creaked open, its hinges groaning in protest as a figure emerged from the darkness. My heart plummeted as my abusive father sauntered in, a smug grin plastered across his face. His eyes were devoid of warmth, glinted with cruel satisfaction, as if he had orchestrated this entire nightmare. "Well, well, well," he sneered, his voice a venomous caress. "Looks like my little pawn has finally made it to the center of the board."

I turned on the cot, facing the cold, blood-stained wall, refusing to grant him the satisfaction of reacting to his remarks.

"Oh, don't be like that, Ezra. After all, you've played your part so well, and soon this will all be over."

My voice was calm, devoid of emotion as I spoke. "Fuck off, Thorin."

His chuckle was a hollow echo in the sterile cell. "Such language from a mother-to-be," he mocked, each word a calculated jab. "But then again, you always were a disappointment, weren't you, Ezra? That's why your mother left you."

His words ignited a spark of fury within me, threatening to consume the fragile control I clung to. "Don't you dare speak of my mother!" I spat, whirling around to face him.

He advanced slowly, each step deliberate and menacing. "Don't think for a moment that being Luna makes any difference here. You will always be that same useless little brat you've always been."

"Maybe, but I'm no longer ignorant of who you are, either, Thorin. I know what you did."

"You think so? Well, I'd love to hear just what it is that you think you know."

"I know you killed my mother."

He didn't confirm it, but he didn't deny it, either. Just looked at me, a smug look on his face, as he veered the conversation to Ayanna. "No matter. Soon, Bash's child will be born, and I will have its power at my disposal." His shadow loomed over me, a suffocating darkness. "Whether you like it or not."

"Bash's child?" I asked, the words laced with disbelief. I knew that Ayanna was his; what I didn't understand was how my father knew that, when I had only just found out myself.

"Oh yes, you see. This was always the plan. Although I'll admit, your slutting around had me worried for a moment there. I hadn't imagined Junior Black would find his way between your legs so quickly. Threatening all these years of planning—of clawing my way to the top, of fawning over that idiot alpha. All the whispers of you I'd put in his ear to ensure the mixing of our bloodlines. All those putrid years of caring for you."

"You call what you did caring for me? You can't actually be serious right now, Thorin. Or are you actually that mental?"

His fist slammed against the metal bedframe in a sudden, violent outburst, the sound reverberating through the cell. "Disrespectful little bitch."

Squaring my shoulders with my abuser, I chuckled before pushing him further. "How do you know this isn't Juno's baby? He is my husband, after all. You don't think I fucked him?"

"Nine weeks ago? Highly doubtful."

My pulse hammered wildly in my chest, a frantic rhythm against the rising tide of panic. Who was the betrayer, the insidious whisperer feeding him details about my child? The realization struck like a physical blow—only the head nurse or her assistant could have known, aside from Juno and me. One of them had to be the traitor.

Thorin's eyes glittered with satisfaction, as if unveiling my secrets brought him some twisted pleasure. "What happens next is up to you. Cooperate, and things can be cordial; however, if you resist or make any attempts to escape me, Ezra, I will be sure to repay the favor in kind."

"What do you want?" I managed, my voice a strained whisper.

Thorin leaned in, his voice a silken threat. "I want what is rightfully mine. The power, the influence you possess…it will belong to me." He paused, his gaze intense. "Hand it over willingly, and I might consider sparing your life. Refuse, and both you and that child will suffer the consequences."

A chill snaked down my spine, colder than any winter wind. "You think you can control me with your threats?" I spat, trying to mask the uncertainty that clawed at my insides. "I'm not afraid of you. Not anymore, and I won't let you touch my child."

Thorin chuckled, a low, humorless sound. "Brave words, Ezra. But bravery is a luxury you can no longer afford. No one is coming to save you." He gestured towards the door, where two hulking figures stood guard. "Consider this your final offer. Choose wisely."

My mind raced, searching for an escape, a loophole, anything. But the shadows pressed in, suffocating me with the weight of his power. I glanced down at my stomach, a silent promise forming in my heart. *I will protect you, no matter the cost.*

"Let me help you."

"Lana," I sighed, feeling comfort in her presence. *"But the baby…"*

"She will be fine, I promise you this. Shift, Ezra. Set me free."

"Alright," I finally agreed. *"I trust you, Lana. What do you want me to do"*

As the oppressive gloom threatened to swallow me, a sudden, primal certainty surged through my veins. Chaos erupted suddenly, and I could feel the pull of something ancient unfurling in my chest, the awakening of power older and fiercer than any of Thorin's schemes. My bones ached, stretching and reforming, and a guttural growl tore from my throat, a sound I didn't recognize as my own.

Thorin's eyes widened in disbelief as my form twisted and contorted, clothes ripping as fur sprouted across my skin. The hulking figures at the door recoiled, fear etching their faces. My first shift was here—a werewolf, born of desperation and defiance.

As Lana took over, it felt like a dam bursting within me, a flood of raw sensations washing away the carefully constructed walls of my human consciousness. My senses sharpened to an almost unbearable degree. The scent of damp earth and distant prey filled my nostrils, overpowering the stale air of the room. Sounds were amplified, the pounding of my own heart a thunderous drumbeat, the rustle of fabric tearing, a deafening roar.

The world exploded with color, vibrant and intense, as if seen through a prism. My muscles coiled and released with newfound power, each movement fluid and instinctive. There was a dizzying rush, a feeling of being untethered from the constraints of my physical form, of being boundless and free.

Yet, amidst the chaos, there was a primal clarity. Lana's instincts were simple, direct: protect, hunt, survive.

All my fears melted away, replaced by a fierce determination, a burning need to defend the precious life growing within me. It was a terrifying, exhilarating surrender, a merging of two souls into something more substantial, something unbreakable. In that moment, I was no longer just Ezra; I was also Lana. And together, we were a force to be reckoned with.

With a roar that shook the very foundations of the room, I lunged. My fangs bared, claws extended, I was no longer the pawn in Juno or Thorin's game. I was something wilder, something dangerous. The battle had begun, and this time, I was playing by a whole new set of rules.

"She's a…a red wolf," one of the guards stuttered.

The Enforcers scattered like mice as I burst through the cell door, a whirlwind of fur and fury. My father stood frozen, disbelief etched on his face, a stark contrast to the terror in the eyes of his henchmen. I spared him only a snarl before leaping forward.

It felt like I was moving on pure instinct. Lana sprinted effortlessly down the corridors, tearing down any wolf who dared to block our escape, to threaten my child.

Minutes later, breaking through the main entrance doors, I leaped into the night.

The forest welcomed me with open arms, the cool earth beneath my paws a balm to my burning skin. I ran, a blur of motion beneath the moonlit canopy, the scent of freedom intoxicating. The Enforcers were fast, but I was faster, driven by a primal instinct to protect the life within me.

The snow crunched under the weight of my wolf as I navigated the dense terrain, the forest floor a familiar path guiding me away from the sterile confines of my father's world. I could hear their shouts in the distance, growing fainter with each stride, their pursuit a futile echo against the symphony of the night.

With a final burst of speed, I reached the edge of the forest. The moon whispered secrets to the night, the wind carried the scent of home, a familiar mix of pine and pack, urging me onward. I burst from the trees, a shadow against the moonlit clearing, and there it was—the pack house, a beacon of warmth and belonging. But as I approached, I saw him: Junior, standing on the porch, his eyes wide set at me.

He'd never seen me like this, never in this form, yet his gaze held a strange fascination. I paused, hesitant, the wolf within me wary of his reaction. Would he recognize the woman beneath the fur?

He took a tentative step forward, his voice barely a whisper. "E"zie?" The sound of my name, spoken with such vulnerability, broke through the primal haze. I lowered my head, offering him a glimpse of the woman he knew, the one hidden beneath the powerful facade. In that moment, I saw the answer in his eyes: understanding, acceptance, and something akin to love.

Juno's POV

A red wolf was a rarity. A creature of legend, symbolizing great power and a deeper connection to ancient magic. They embodied the spirit of fire and passion, and were believed to possess unique abilities and a heightened sense of intuition, making them revered and respected among werewolves.

I had never seen one, not in all my years. I had no idea that Ezra's wolf would match the fiery essence of all that she was, her strength and resilience. But I knew, instantly, that the wolf standing before me was her. It was no wonder she survived the death of her mate. Her wolf was far from ordinary.

I was helplessly drawn, unable to look away. She was more than a dream, more than a hope. I thought once, she might be my salvation. Now, I knew her purpose was infinitely grander compared to my own selfish reprieve.

We had been preparing to breach the Enforcers' compound, to liberate her, yet there she was, a vision in the wild. *Had she escaped that fortress alone?* My body moved without command, the world a blur, the pounding of my heart a drum in my ears. My vision tunneled, focusing on Ezra, her wolf a beacon in the night, drawing me irresistibly closer. Each step was an eternity, closing the distance between our souls.

As I drew closer, Ezra's wolf tilted her head, her eyes—pools of molten gold—locking onto mine. A low, guttural rumble resonated from her chest, not a threat, but a recognition, a question. My hand reached out, trembling, drawn by an invisible cord.

"Ezra? Come back to me," I whispered, my voice barely audible above the frantic rhythm of my heart.

The wolf took a step forward, closing the remaining space between us. Her massive head lowered, nudging my outstretched hand. The fur beneath my fingertips was warm, vibrant, pulsing with an energy that sent shivers down my spine.

In that moment, the world dissolved. The Enforcers, the compound, my own fears—all faded into insignificance. There was only Ezra, her wolf, and the silent understanding that passed between us. She was never a damsel to be rescued, but a force of nature, a beacon of strength.

A shift rippled through her form, a graceful undulation of muscle and bone. The red wolf shimmered, resolving into the beautiful silhouette of her, my little one, my dolly, my Luna. Though forever changed. Her icy blue eyes held the same fiery intensity as her wolf, but now, there was a quiet power that radiated from her very being.

"Honey, I'm home," she said, her voice a husky whisper, imbued with the wildness of the wolf. "And now, we have two wars to win.